"With no money and another author's work, Whedon finds his strength in the superb cast, clever staging, and an expert understanding of dialogue" – *Collider*

"There's joy bubbling under everything, and the film is at its best when it lets that joy out" – *Hitfix.com*

"Whedon fans? They'll gush over this like Claudio writing a gooey love sonnet to Hero" – *Film.com*

"The result is an utter joy" – *Indiewire*

"A wholly unexpected, what-the-hell passion project... it's pretty inspiring" – *Variety*

"This is the funniest Shakespeare film I can recall seeing" – *NewYorkPost.com*

"A faithful yet modern adaptation" – *Splashpage*

"Seeing [Joss Whedon] interpret and adapt the Bard is sure to be a treat" – *Yahoo Movies Canada*

"The film radiates such love and passion, light and meaty in equal measure, it's a joy to watch" – *DailyBlam*

"I believe the comedy and I believe the romance" – *CraveOnline.com*

"It is vibrant and bubbly and just clever enough to engage people who wouldn't normally watch a black-and-white micro-budget Shakespeare adaptation" – *Film.com*

"The best part of Joss Whedon's adaptation of Much Ado About Nothing is probably when Fred and Wesley finally get to be happy together despite the villainous machinations of Simon Tam" – *AVClub.com*

"A labour of love devoted to the Bard" – *Reuters*

"An engaging and very funny adaptation of the William Shakespeare classic" – *CinemaBlend.com*

"The affection with which it's been produced is cont

D1019199

MUCH ADO ABOUT NOTHING

A film by
Joss Whedon

MUCH ADO ABOUT NOTHING:
A FILM BY JOSS WHEDON
ISBN: 9781781169353

Published by
Titan Books
A division of Titan Publishing Group Ltd.
144 Southwark St.
London
SE1 0UP

First edition: October 2013
10 9 8 7 6 5 4 3 2 1

All photographs taken by Elsa Guillet-Chapuis.

Special thanks to Abbie Bernstein for conducting the interviews.

Did you enjoy this book? We love to hear from our readers. Please e-mail us at:
readerfeedback@titanemail.com or write to Reader Feedback at the above address.

To receive advance information, news, competitions, and exclusive offers online, please sign
up for the Titan newsletter on our website: **www.titanbooks.com**

A CIP catalogue record for this title is available from the British Library.

Printed and bound in the USA.

More Joss Whedon titles from Titan Books:

Dr Horrible's Sing-Along Blog: The Book
Firefly: The Official Companion Vol 1-2
The Cabin in the Woods: The Official Visual Companion

MUCH ADO ABOUT NOTHING

A film by
Joss Whedon

BASED ON THE PLAY BY
WILLIAM SHAKESPEARE

Bellwether Pictures

TITAN BOOKS

CONTENTS

MUCH ADO ABOUT NOTHING
AN INTRODUCTION BY
JOSS WHEDON

Some things I just don't get. I don't understand how they work. Gun lobbyists. Gluten. Human decency. All confusing on many levels.

Things I do understand: Art. Food (gluten notwithstanding). Whining.

Above all, the thing I've never cracked, after decades of being, embarrassingly, obsessed with the subject, is me. The most obvious things about me pass me right by. When I find them out, long after everyone else has, I usually find I've been writing about them. For years. Thinking I wasn't writing about me -- thinking any artist is ever expressing anything other than themselves.

I don't remember deciding to film **Much Ado About Nothing**. I remember Kai telling me I should – telling me, wisely, that I needed to. A month later I was, and my world, usually black and white, resounded with joyous color. It was so bright, so right, so extraordinary an experience that it seemed disconnected from everything before and everything after. But what made it so great was **only** connection, was only the past, the past that had been pushing me to make this movie, just this one, since before I was born. By about 400 years.

Let's start there. (I'm supposed to say something nice about the writer. It's a thing.) Every artist expresses themselves, but a few find themselves speaking for everyone, and they tend to be remembered. Shakespeare's plays have been a passion of mine since I was old enough to have passions. Not terribly original, but blame the Bard for that. These stories, verses, words... they're indelible. There's a distance from the norm – 400 years will do that, plus the conventions of the form – that makes the plays work as pure poetry, as a lost language, as music. But there's an intimacy and insight that makes that music stick, and stick, through centuries. He's writing about us, duh. Even when it appears that he's writing about nothing.

(That's what stopped me. For years. Those two words. I had never studied the text, just enjoyed it. Watched Amy and Alexis dominate that text during a reading at the house, dreamed of shooting them doing it, but always falling back. Not for me. I like stories with a message, an intent. I have nothing to say about nothing.)

The readings. They started with my mother (maybe my father was involved, but by the time my memory works it's my stepfather beside her). Thanksgiving, every year: Shakespeare, Shaw, Wilde, Kaufman... light fare, before the heavier stuff was carved and served.

They started again when James Marsters remarked that doing a particular ep of *Buffy the Vampire Slayer* was like being in rep. That made me realize that I was surrounded by actors and theater geeks, many of whom understood Shakespeare on levels I never would, and that we ought to celebrate that somehow. We met on Sundays. We read, we drank (less when we got over our initial fear, and way less than the people in this movie) we sang, we talked – we got a good ways through the canon before babies came into the picture and the group went fallow. I was made aware, again and again, what a remarkable bunch of thesps I had at my beck. Kai and I discussed taping the readings – something to put on the internet, perhaps, for schools – but the ephemeral intimacy of the readings was half their charm, and plus it sounded like work. We decided, if we were going to film one, we'd **film** it.

Then Kai built a house.

The most inviting, **involving** home I've ever been in, let alone lived in. An architect is just like a filmmaker: we create moments for people to move through, strung together to make that movement feel like more than just passage. It's not the wall, it's how you see the wall, what's on it, what it does with the light, what it feels like when you walk by it. I knew I wanted to film the house the moment it was finished. It was, among so many other things, the perfect set.

So I had the actors, the location, the tiny budget, the wonderful text... Kai even had a crew in place. My whole career – a large part of my life – had been laying the groundwork for this. What kept me from making a movie?

Nothing. Still with the "nothing".

I don't remember figuring it out. I walked across the street from the rubbled Manhattan *Avengers* location and bought a copy of the play (actually, Danny bought it. My wallet was in my trailer. I still haven't paid him back. I never will! Suck it, Kaminsky!) and then it was in my pocket, and then it was in my head, and then I had the movie and the rest is a footnote in history. Thinking that the play was actually about nothing is like complaining that the titular character never shows up in *Waiting For Godot*. (Spoiler alert: he doesn't show.) There was so much **something** in the text, not just between Beatrice and Benedick but with everyone (except Antonio. Sorry, bro – couldn't crack ya), so much life and pain and duplicity and pain and such high-pain-jinks, there was no way I couldn't film it. This was the most cynically romantic piece I'd read. It completely obliterated the tropes of romantic love, while ultimately championing love itself. This was me talking about me. This was meat. I was in.

It only took 400 years for me to figure it out.

JOSS WHEDON

WITHOUT FURTHER ADO...
AN INTERVIEW WITH
JOSS WHEDON

What, if anything, was your experience of theatre before you saw Shakespeare?

My mother directed summer stock in Dennis on Cape Cod [Massachusetts]. Literally, my first memories are of being around that theatre. My dad wrote off-off-Broadway stuff and both my godmother and godfather were actors, and all we listened to [Steven] Sondheim shows my entire childhood. Theatre has just always been in my life.

What was your first experience of Shakespeare?

I don't remember my first experience with Shakespeare. The first really great times I had were at [Shakespeare] readings, when we'd read a play. I'd say my favorite memory, when we'd read a play with my mother and stepfather, and honestly, my favorite memory of young adolescence, was getting to play Hal to my stepfather's Falstaff in *Henry IV: Part I* and thereby getting to call him fat for three pages, which was something I liked to do anyway. That was just a joy.

What was your first reaction to Shakespearean language?

I made my way through it. I remember reading the *Henrys* probably too early and just kind of trudging my way through and looking up everything [laughs], reading an extended footnote, because all the words were so new to me. And gradually becoming more conversant and gradually seeing a lot there that I enjoyed and a lot there that I wouldn't until I saw it performed. It was definitely a bit of an effort at first. Then when I got to England and really got to see, not just great performances, but sort of *offhand* great performances, like, 'Oh, we just do this. We just toss one of these off.' And working with amazing teachers. That's when it really unfolded.

Do you remember when you first saw a production of *Much Ado About Nothing*?
Yeah. It was at the open-air theatre in Regent's Park in London, and it completely floored me, because it was so funny. I mean, that really was the thing – it was just hilarious. I saw it three times. They were doing *Midsummer* in rep[ertory], I saw that three times. I was astonished how accessible it was and how over the top it was. Some of that was in the staging, but the moment they finished the hilarious gulling scene, when the first words out of Benedick's mouth are, 'This can be no trick!' I lost it. I was like, 'I can't believe he went there, that is just absurd.' The sort of deeper meanings of the thing? Lost on me. The feminist aspect of it? Lost on me. What I remember from that production was just laughing my ass off.

What to you is the big difference, if any, between filmed Shakespeare and staged Shakespeare?
I've never directed theatre really, so I would just say, filmed Shakespeare [calls for] a different set of tools. Theatre is something that is alive – you're watching living people. A bad production of Shakespeare might make you think that they are dead, and they're creaking around like zombies, but very articulate zombies. But film has to capture the electricity that is created between these characters, without having that actual proximity [to live actors] and that makes it tough, but it has cinema. It has an enormous amount of visual language the ability to back the words up in a way that the theatre doesn't, so part of it is about translation, it's about making sure that you're using the camera, you're using every cinematic trick you have to augment the emotionality of the thing, because you have lost the frisson of personal [live] involvement.

What is your favorite Shakespeare play?
It's *Hamlet*.

Is that your favorite scripted text?
Yeah. It's *Hamlet*, for the love of God. It's hard to argue with. Especially if you're an alienated teen, and then years after you're an alienated teen, nobody tells you that you're not any more [laughs].

When and why did you start doing readings of Shakespeare plays at your home with your actor friends?

I started doing them because we were shooting Episode Seven of Season Five of *Buffy*. It was James Marsters, who'd been [as Spike] playing a punk on a subway and then playing a bad nineteenth-century poet, and he said, 'This reminds me of being in rep.' And that just made something click, and I thought back to the readings we'd had when I was a kid, which we'd do once a year. And I just thought, 'You know what? What if a bunch of us got together and read some of the plays of a Sunday?' And it just kind of didn't stop.

Did you direct the readings at your house?
Not in the sense of ever saying, 'Do it this way.' The thing about the readings was, people just showed up and had their fun. The only directing I did was, if we ever did *Midsummer [Night's Dream]*, I would make them stand up in front of everyone to do 'Pyramus and Thisbe.'

Fran Kranz, who plays Claudio in *Much Ado*, has talked about working with Alan Tudyk in 'Pyramus and Thisbe' at one of the *Midsummer* readings at your house. Alexis Denisof was Wall ...
I think [Tudyk] was Bottom in that production. Fran was Thisbe [laughs]. I know that Sarah Vowell was the Lion, because honestly, who better to play a lion?

You're in a different house now than you were when you started doing those readings?
Yes, but that reading of "Midsummer" was at the new house.

Your wife Kai Cole is the architect who designed your current home. Was the house designed to be filmed in?
You know, it wasn't designed to be filmed in, in the sense of, 'Let's make a fake house' [laughs]. It was designed in the sense to be spacious and to have flow and to be lovely. It wasn't designed so that there'd be enough room to get a camera back in the corner, but by God, there is. We wanted particularly to make a creative space. And all her creative use of space in, 'Let's connect these rooms – oh, let's take this, let's make a little secret attic-y space out of this where these walls connect, where these rooms connect, that the kids can crawl through.' She wanted the experience of the space to be varied. And there's a little dance studio downstairs that is in fact where Verges [Tom Lenk] and Dogberry [Nathan Fillion] have their scenes, and there's a potting wheel and there's a tiny recording space. We wanted to encourage people to come and just do artistic [endeavors] – we wanted our kids to be around as much art and life, and this was something that both of us were very committed to, and this was another big part of my childhood. My mom had what we referred to as 'the community,' which was a pseudo-commune that we did several summers in a row at the farm upstate when she wasn't teaching. We'd all live up there and

get a bunch of families and there'd be a bunch of her friends, students, artists... Poetry reading to harp accompaniment – did we rock that? Yes, we rocked that. So the idea of this eclectic, artistic space was important. One of the first times we got to pay that off was when our friend wanted to put on a play. They couldn't do it [at a traditional theatre], and so we invited the cast to do it at our house and opened up the family room, which they used as the set at one end and basically just opened up the French doors, lined up a bunch of chairs and they got to do their play. But more importantly, for three weeks, the kids got to come home from school and watch them rehearse their play, and them being around that was just so exciting, and I think that was another sort of door being unlocked for us, going, 'You know what? We can film here.'

When Kai came to you and said, 'Let's do this instead of taking a vacation in Italy,' was 'this' specifically *Much Ado*?

It was *Much Ado*. Because we had talked about it for so long and because *Much Ado* worked for us in every practical way. We had our stars, it's all on one location and we knew that the house was perfect for that location, so those problems are solved. We knew we had everything. The only resistance I had was [clenched whisper], 'I don't have a take on the text. I don't have a movie. I can film a play, but I don't have a movie.' And a production, let alone a movie, without a point of view is inevitably soggy. You can always tell when someone is just throwing a bunch of tricks up on the stage because it's time to do that play and they don't really have an idea beyond that. But it probably took thirty minutes of reading, of [Kai] saying, 'Well, look at the text and just see, because everything's in place – see if there's something you missed.' And thirty minutes later, 'Oh, I got it.'

Can you articulate what 'it' is?

The 'it' is the understanding that everything in the play is an important part of the play, that all of the relationships and all of the schemes and all of the plot devices have equal weight. Inevitably, *Much Ado* is played as a two-hander. It's 'Beatrice and Benedick, and if you can make it through the wedding scene, they'll be right back.' And to me, who Claudio is and who Hero is and what Leonato's going through and Don Pedro and Margaret and Ursula – everybody, particularly Borachio, has a part of what this movie is about, and when you give yourself up to them and invest equal weight in all of these characters, you really have something that's more than the sum of its parts, something that's dark, something that's not necessarily as charming as it appears to be, but ultimately very romantic, and that's what hit me, that's what made me go, 'Oh! He says it's 'about nothing' because he's tricking me.' And I know it's a dirty Elizabethan pun, but also, he's saying something very specific with the word 'nothing,' which I had overlooked.

What is the dirty Elizabethan pun?

Much Ado About an O-Thing, which is a womanly place. And it's also 'noting.' 'Nothing' was supposed to be a homonym for 'noting,' and it's all about people sort of observing each other, so there's a lot going on with the title. [I was] completely unaware of any of this. And at the end of the day, there may have been opportunities missed; dirty puns was one of them. Although – movie dirty, so clearly I got the intent.

How much of the impetus to film a Shakespeare play at your house was because you wanted the experience of filming a Shakespeare play at your house, how much was because you wanted to do this particular production of *Much Ado About Nothing*, and how much was because you wanted to see what it looked like when it was done?

I filmed the movie because Kai and I had started Bellwether [their production company, which made *Much Ado*] as a micro studio, because we'd had such a good experience with *Dr. Horrible*. We started [Bellwether] before, but particularly after *Avengers*, we wanted to do things on that smaller scale, do things that were not beholden to anything but our own indie imaginations. So it was Kai who insisted at the end of the *Avengers* shoot that I take our anniversary trip to Venice and turn it to a trip to Messina [where *Much Ado* is set] instead. She said, 'I have a crew in place, you need to do this, it will make you better. And Venice isn't sinking that fact.' [laughs]. And obviously it was absurdly medicinal. But it really just had to do with wanting to do things that we loved with the people we loved in the way that we really enjoy, which is down and dirty, run 'n' gun, just sort of hit that electricity of, 'Good God, we're really puttin' on a show, and practically using the old barn.' And the only way to do that was to use a script that was already really good, and finished.

It has been pointed out that *Much Ado* has more prose and less verse than anything else in the Shakespeare canon. Did that have anything to do with your choice?

Honestly, I would say yes, but I didn't notice it until we were rehearsing. I was like [extremely upper-class East Coast accent], 'So, where's the verse?' I do think that one of the reasons it appeals and one of the reasons why I thought it would be not just a good film but a good gateway drug for Shakespeare is that it's so relatable and it's so modern and a lot of that has to do with those rhythms. I had noticed that forcibly when playing Iago to J. August Richards' Othello, how the conversations between them are ridiculously modern in their rhythms. I had sort of missed the fact that really, apart from what's sung, there's pretty much no verse at all in *Much Ado*. But I do think that makes it much easier to present to a modern audience.

Along those lines, what do you feel you're saying about *Much Ado* or bringing out of it that hasn't come out before? At least on film – no one, unless they're Doctor Who, could possibly have seen every stage production of it that's ever been …

Yeah, and everything you could ever say or do somebody's said or done. Usually by Shakespeare, and usually better. But for me, every production is a chance for somebody to insert themselves, the way an actor does into a role. And that's not to say, not to improve Shakespeare or to outsmart him – because I've seen productions that try to do that, too – but to bring what theatre requires, which is your own sensibility, and what film requires. And for me, what forcibly hit me was the darkness, the cynicism, the way it plays off the comedy. I'm a big fan of certain noir comedies, like *The Apartment* and *Unfaithfully Yours*, and this was both in equal measure. To me, it felt like Shakespeare was deconstructing the romantic comedy while he was inventing it. The entire thing takes everything we understand about love and behaviors and our rituals, and basically says, 'It's all societal construct, it's a game.' And the victory is for Beatrice and Benedick to stop playing the game and just admit that they have decided to need each other and that their love works because of that, because they've grown up past what's expected of them.

When you were doing the adaptation of the script, how did you decide what to keep and what to cut from the original text?

The play is very long. And I had to cut out at least a third of it. I mean, the gulling scene alone – it's twice as long as what's in the film. Inevitably, you do make cuts. What's great is, every time you do it, you might do it differently than the guy before. So it's kind of like a menu, especially in that scene. 'Well, how would you like the scene to play? Because he wrote it three times, and it's all there' [laughs]. There are also scenes where they're explaining something that you just saw and that's what Antonio fell victim to. Leonato's brother I ousted, because he was one character where I wasn't able to find how he was bringing anything that was other than exposition or support, so he went buh-bye. And then I took the two messengers and a bit from Balthasar and combined them all into Leonato's aide, who Josh Zar plays, because I wanted to convey the man of import, and the man of import always has the other man standing behind him and it made sense to track this through as a character in the film rather than just have a bunch of messengers appear.

Is there anything that you de-emphasized?

Well, there are a lot of complaints that are very justified about the play, about the conflict hinging on whether or not Hero is a virgin, and that she has given up her maidenhead. And to me, the story there, the part that works, the part where we still want to watch this play, isn't that Claudio thinks she's not a virgin, it's that he thinks she's cheating on him. It's jealousy, which is universal and very modern. It's not about propriety. When Claudio turns on her at the wedding, it's because he thinks she's making a fool of him, he thinks she's sleeping with somebody else the night before her wedding. That's *never* okay. And when [Hero's father]

Leonato goes at her, he's particularly brutal. Clark and I had a lot of trouble with that. What we were talking about there was his humiliation in front of all of his peers and his betrayal by the most important person in his life. There's no mother in the family, it's just him and her. So for her to have been lying to him is heartbreaking for him. And Hero, who just sort of wilts – even though she was going to faint, it's an important plot point, I wanted very much for her to meet this head on, rather than just go [dazed voice], 'What's going on? Why are people so – I'm just gonna lie down now.' It was important for me to say, 'Okay, this is a strong girl' – I mean, Hero is the only person in the whole play who never believes something that's not true. It's not an enormous part, but it doesn't have to be this pathetic little wilty flower, and that's part of the reason that I cast Jillian [Morgese as Hero], is that there's a strength there. This is why I had Hero watching the funeral procession, because in order for her to forgive Claudio, I wanted her to see that he was showing true remorse.

When you were watching Amy Acker play Beatrice and Alexis Denisof play Benedick in the *Much Ado* readings at your home, did you immediately think, 'Must film them doing this at some point,' or did you just think, 'If I ever *do* film this, I want them'?
Yeah. I'm very big with the, 'Hey! Let's all do this thing that I totally think I have time to do 'cause I'm drunk.' The pasts of my friends are littered with promises that I wasn't able to keep. But I knew I wanted to film [Acker and Denisof] doing that – I thought that would be great. I didn't really pursue it, though, because every time I thought about it, which was a lot, I kept bumping up against my lack of understanding of the text. And all that it took for me to fix that was for me to look at the damn thing. But in my head, I had one idea in mind, and it had probably been formed from that first production [seen in Regent's Park], which was, the 'about nothing' of it, that it was just a charming romp. Which for me to think that, to be stuck in that, is appalling. Because I'd studied the [Shakespearean] Comedies as well. Not that one, but it was very clear to me that they were very important works, and that he [Shakespeare] didn't just throw in meaning when he had a tragedy. That's an easy mistake to make, but as far as *Much Ado*, I just didn't really see what it was. And I think another sort of tumbler in that lock was, I saw a production of it at the Kirk Douglas [a live stage theatre in the Los Angeles area] the year before and Dakin Matthews played Leonato. And he was a very sort of bumbling Leonato. The performance was just hilarious and riveting and your heart just broke during the wedding scene when he's yelling at his daughter, because the weight of the thing is all on him. And it's a very different interpretation than Clark and I went for, but it sort of made me go, 'Wait a minute, this whole play's about Leonato.' And that made me want to go back in: 'Now wait a minute. Let me look more carefully at not just the text, but all of these characters, because clearly there's meat there that I wasn't seeing.'

Were there any other readings where you thought, 'I'd really like to use this cast on film?'

There was a bunch. I mean, we're talking about a swell bunch of thesps and there were definitely some that I was just like [admiringly], 'Oh ...' But I don't think there was one that I had as strong a feeling about as *Much Ado*, because Amy and Alexis, they displayed just such versatility and charisma in every reading, it blew everybody away. We tried very hard to have an egalitarian troupe, but they really turned out to be rock stars. And so, besides the fact that I love them dearly, pairing the two of them, which has been a habit of mine [laughs], just made something work for me that nothing else captured.

Denisof and Acker played, respectively, Wesley and Fred for you on Angel; the characters wound up as star-crossed tragic lovers. Did you have any thoughts about how Wesley/Fred fans would react on seeing the two actors like this in Much Ado?

Not until literally screening it. And not even the first time. It was a couple of months ago, screening it, I suddenly went, 'Oh, my God! Wesley and Fred went to Heaven and they got this! They're kissing and neither of them is dying! This is delightful.' There's a reason why I throw those two actors into each other's arms every chance I get.

Why did you decide to show that Beatrice and Benedick had been lovers previous to the main events in the film?

The idea that Beatrice and Benedick have slept together before the action of the play is a modern one, I think, but it seems entirely valid — it doesn't undermine the text. Amy and Alexis and I all agreed we wanted to play this version that way because it puts heat into their animosity, and fits the sort of debauched hothouse intensity of this particular production. The idea wasn't just that they'd had a one night stand, but that something really meaningful, really open, had happened and they'd both clammed up right away — afraid of it. And then each resenting the other for it.

That's the only bit not shot at the house — it was shot at my office bungalow nearby, and we did paint the walls a dark plum to make it different from Leonato's. Then I liked the color and kept it.

Was there anything besides casting Denisof and Acker that you took from the *Much Ado* house readings that has turned up in the film, or anything you learned from the readings that you said, 'Must not do this in the film'?

Cast myself [laughs]. And the songs. I had written the songs -- or the tunes -- for that reading, and we sort of surprised everybody with them. I had cast our singer friend Angie Hart as Balthasar and when it came time for Balthasar to sing, her husband whipped out a guitar, my brother Sam whipped out his mandolin, and off to the races, which was really fun, because we brought it up a notch with that. And those are the tunes that we use in the film, but there were a couple of things, just attitudes and pauses and little things that I know Alexis did that I said, 'Oh, that's funnier than it was when I read it in my head.' But there weren't a lot of dos and don'ts. That was a sort of Branagh-like experience [a reference to Kenneth Branagh's 1993 film version of *Much Ado About Nothing*], in that we were out in the back and there were sun-dappled vines and a general air of joy and kind of sunny good times and when I looked at the movie as a movie, I realized that that wasn't the sort of overriding emotion that I was trying to evoke.

How much of this *Much Ado* was pre-cast and how much was, 'Who would be good in this?' and how much was, 'I'm going to use people I haven't really worked with before'?

You know, two parts [Beatrice and Benedick] were pre-cast [laughs]. And the next thing on my list was, 'Oh, I really want Nathan [Fillion] to play Dogberry.' Pompous and clueless – Nathan, I think his first time reading Shakespeare was at the house. And he read Bottom. And the naturalism that he brought to that guy was just gut-bustingly funny, but also a little dazzling, so I was like, 'Okay, that's the next thing I'm going for.' And then I made a list, I wrote it on the cast list – 'This person I asked, they're working, well, what about this person? What about this person? What about this person?' And then I came home and started feeling people out. I always had more than one option, because you never knew who was going to be available, but I really didn't ever have to settle. And I had a strong feeling about Jillian [who was an extra in *Avengers*] – after a couple of weeks back in L.A. I auditioned her on Skype and said, 'Okay, that's how it's going to be.' And then some people like Riki I knew just a little bit, but was a fan of, and Nick [Kocher as First Watchman] and Brian [McElhaney as Second Watchman – Kocher and McElhaney are a comedy duo] I didn't know at all but was a fan of, just reached out to them, thought, 'Maybe ...' But I kept it fairly fluid. I came home and I had a coming-home party, because I'd been away in Albuquerque shooting *Avengers* for the better part of a year. At the party, I just sort of said to everybody [very casual tone of voice], 'So, what you doin'? So, what you up to? On what dates? Okay, yeah ...' I mean, I was not so subtle [laughs], but it was a way of feeling everybody out, because what I didn't want to do was suddenly end up with, 'Oh, good, I have five people that I've found out are available for this part. Oh, wait a minute, four of them are going to hate me.' So I just sort of got a sense of who was available. And we also had to work around people's schedules, because most people were working anyway.

Nathan Fillion has said he had gotten so scared of doing Shakespeare that he tried to get out of the project ...

Yeah, he was very nervous about it, whether he could pull this off. And he was working crazy *Castle* hours, because *Castle* is built on the shoulders of him. He tried to plead overwork, and I said, 'Okay, look, I'll take you out of the first scene where I put you in and you have no lines, and I can do some trims on the other stuff so we can get it into your schedule, but dude, you're coming. You're not saying "no".'

How do you pronounce Jillian Morgese's last name?
Mor-*jess*-ee.

Can you talk about choosing her to play Hero?
She's absurdly beautiful, but it's not like I lack for beautiful ingénues in my troupe. Why Jillian struck me as Hero particularly is that she felt like a very good match for Amy [Hero and Beatrice are cousins]. They're both very tall, very poised and have fabulous noses. They felt like they would fit together in a way that didn't feel like casting. They felt like family to me. Jillian has a great deal of self-possession and a kind of strength that you wouldn't notice at first. And Amy is the same way. Plus Jillian had to do a lot of freaking out and crying in *Avengers,* so I knew she could get there and get there quickly. She actually told me she had taken a 'Law & Order' class -- it's a New York thing. Lotta crying.

Can you talk about Hero and Claudio as characters?
I feel like Hero is underserved in the same way that Claudio is. People just say, 'Okay, be pretty – and now be sad – don't talk too much.' Their romance is problematic to say the least, even at its conclusion, and I wanted to do everything in my power to make those parts interesting. I think Claudio very often gets played as kind of wet. And I'm like, 'Ah, this is a decorated soldier. He's a tough guy.' And here he is – he believes everything he hears, and he gets really angry about it, he's got a temper, he's not so bright maybe [laughs], but what he *isn't* is a wimp. He's something entirely different. It's clear that he's a much better soldier than Benedick, and the fun of it with Fran was, first of all, he is extraordinary. People don't think of Fran certainly as the jock type, unless they've seen him with his shirt off, but to cast somebody who's as gently appealing as Fran and then have him play as somebody who is darkly hot-tempered and occasionally so obtuse that it's hilarious – Fran's usually the guy who knows everything in my work [Topher in *Dollhouse* and Marty in *Cabin in the Woods*], and so that was fun for him to try and, 'Can I dig less deep? Can I be maybe more of a dick?' [laughs] But again, to say, 'Okay, Claudio is the guy with a history that makes him do what he does.' And that's more interesting than, again [whining], 'Oh, my, I'm so, so sad ...'

Is Reed Diamond as Don Pedro the actor you talked about in another interview, saying you couldn't tell if he was starting to say his dialogue for the scene or if he was just chatting, because he was so natural?

I would say that was probably Reed. Reed is a rock star, and he had never done one of the readings, but I knew he was a Juilliard boy, and he and I, we love to fop, and we can fop for hours on end. I'm amazed anybody is still talking to us, because we would just go on and on. He really is way too much fun. But that's obviously not how he performed it [laughs]. I call out Reed particularly, because when we got to, 'We are the only love gods,' it was getting late. We'd been in that kitchen for a long time. We came around to his side [to get the camera angle favoring Diamond for the scene] and I was like, 'This is going to be really rough, it's going to be a very long day,' because we still had a page of stuff, mostly his, and then, bam -- one take. He nailed it on the first take, and I was like, 'Thank you for that extra hour that I got back!'

Did you find yourself working at all differently with the actors who were familiar with Shakespeare versus the ones who were new to Elizabethan dialogue?

You know, it's interesting. There were a couple of people that I worked with a little harder than others. It was very seldom about the language, though. With Jillian, sometimes I would go over the specificity of what she was saying, so that it didn't get lost in just musical-sounding language. But the most work I did with Jillian was on trying to teach her how to do a spit take. And with Tom Lenk, again, language wasn't a problem, but he hasn't played a lot of cops. And so my big note to Tom would be, after a take, 'Tom, what's it like on the beat?' And he'd go, 'It's tough on the beat.' 'Okay, we're going again.' Just to get, 'I want world-weary cop. I want that guy.' But it was interesting to me that the adjustments that I was making almost never were about speech. But there were some moments when someone said, 'Well, what exactly – why am I saying it this way? How do I refer to this there?' And I would just say [summoning him], 'Alexis, please!'

So Alexis Denisof was your on-set Shakespearean resource?

I didn't mean for that to be, but I would find that the way I had studied the text had been purely through an emotional lens. Apart from a basic understanding of what people were saying, I didn't find out – I didn't research the play. I didn't find out about the apparently dirty Elizabethan pun in the title until a couple of weeks ago.

Did any of the actors have any confusion as to the exact nature of the project?

I definitely had one or two people say they expected to just show up on the day and have me with my [camera] phone, going, 'Action!' But I think by the time Maileen Williams, the first a.d., had contacted everybody enough times, they had sort of begun to realize this wasn't just a home movie.

Why did you decide to shoot the film in black and white?

Because I saw this as sort of a noir comedy, the movies that I thought of as connecting to it were the older movies, black and white movies. I toyed with the idea for a few reasons, one of which is, I thought it would have the right kind of timeless elegance and take care of any weird glaring color issues that I couldn't control. It would work better for the house, the way people would stand out against the walls, which were all quite light, would pop better in black and white, and I thought that was going to be important, because I couldn't paint the whole house – I mean, I probably could've, but I didn't want to. And I talked to Kai about it, and I said, 'I'm going back and forth, because there are a lot of beautiful colors, and it's a big decision.' And as soon as I told her about it, she said, 'Oh, no, it's black and white. No, no, no, that conversation's over. It has to be – it will look so great.' It was another way of separating it [from the Branagh version], because we've got a lot of sun out here, and rolling green hills and mountains, and again, I didn't want to try to make what Branagh had already made. And there's a beauty to it that is inexpressible. There's also a coldness to it, and that's me.

Joss Whedon, beautiful but cold.

I'm just sayin'.

How did you decide on the film's budget?

Pretty much by finding out what the least amount of money that there has ever been would be.

Was it like, 'These are the things we cannot do without, how much do they cost, that's the budget'?

Pretty much, yeah. I mean, 'We've got to work with the unions and we've got to provide certain things and we're going to need a few cameras, because there's no way this gets done with just one, and we need a lighting package. The main component of our lighting package rises in the east and sets in the west, but we need to augment that.' There is a whole micro-budget world that Kai had begun to investigate for Bellwether, for another project [*In Your Eyes*]. Because when we did *Dr. Horrible*, there were a lot of favors and a lot of people who don't do that sort of supermax low-budget kind of thing, but there are people out there who specialize in it, and we got together a crew and line producers and a.d.s that just understood that structure and that method and that speed better than anybody I've worked with, but they also understood the movie we were trying to make. They became family as fast as anyone, which is a glorious thing.

What was the scene that was shot over two days?

This is another reason for the black and white, because you can mix color temperatures willy-nilly. It was the one time we ran out of day. In the scene when all has been resolved and Benedick comes to Friar Francis [Paul Meston] and says, 'I want to get married.' The girls are upstairs putting on their veils – that's where Hero does her 'Daddy, stop picking on Margaret' moment. And Leonato comes downstairs and stands with the Friar. All of that was shot at night with us pumping light in through the various windows and doors that would have been just out of frame. But it was too late to shoot the living room, the reverse, because there was no way we could take all those big windows and pretend it was daytime. So Benedick's side of the shot [was done] the following week with Clark standing there by the camera. Paul had actually already gone back to England. But that's one of those things where black and white just saved our lives. Matching those two things would have been impossible with the kind of package we had, but [director of photography] Jay Hunter, did such beautiful work so simply – a tiny bit of which got lost in the IT. The [digital] files disappeared for a little of the stuff of Claudio getting out of the pool and Benedick coming up to him – there are a couple of very gorgeous shots that just disappeared. After Margaret walks downstairs, I had been meaning to take Benedick out to the balcony for his balcony scene, because the balcony is right there, and any time that I can connect spaces, I like to do that, so you see, 'Oh, God, that really is an environment.' I was about to do that. They said, 'We just lost footage.' And we had to run downstairs and shoot Fran getting out of the pool again – not the entire pool scene, just him getting out, doing his whole internal monologue, and then we'd also lost a beautiful shot of Alexis walking in the house with the sun behind him. And it was never replicated.

Is it true that your director of photography Jay Hunter apparently hit himself with the face with a piece of camera equipment and was blind in one eye for a couple of days?
He did that. As a true maverick should, he had a rig where he could hold the camera on a sort of string. You've got the rig over your shoulder, the string comes down and the camera hangs from that, so he could get low-angle shots while walking, particularly when he was trying to get Leonato coming out of the house to get angry at everybody about his dead daughter, and I wanted to be low on Clark when he walked out of the house. And while we were doing it, the cord thing, which was pulled taut, snapped off the camera and into [Hunter's] eye. He of course just slapped on a bandage – 'Let's go, I'm fine.' Blood was pouring down. We were like [worried tone], 'Maybe you're not ...' 'It's good.'

Is there any detectable difference in the footage shot while he didn't have use of the eye?
Yes – the 3D is not nearly as effective.

You reportedly had to contend with a lot of sound issues, including barking dogs and lawnmowers from the golf course and house construction.

We sure did. They actually started construction – they started demoing the house next door three days before we started shooting, the house next door to us.

How did you deal with that?

Through sheer panic. Kai just said, 'I'll go and fix it. I'll get them to stop.' I said, 'I don't think that you can. I think you think you an but I don't think you can.' And she came back a couple hours later and said, 'They're going to stop work whenever we shoot. Who's your producer?'

Is it true that some of your neighbors called the cops?

Yes, bless their hearts. During the wedding scene, people got a little bit, I'm sorry to say, lax with the parking. We had told them not to park on the street and somebody complained that there were too many cars parked on the street. A cop came and said, 'Well, you need a permit for this.' 'It's our home.' 'Well, I'm going to shut you down.' And it was in the middle of the wedding scene, right before Hero and Leonato tangle, for all of their big stuff. So the cop went away and we kept shooting. And Kai rushed downtown to discover that, as we thought, we did not need a permit. We just signed a thing and it was all fine. But those were tense moments. The noise, the cop – that stuff gave me a stomach ache. I was like, 'Maybe we should wait, let's break for lunch,' and Clark was just like, 'No. I'm ready to go. Are you kidding?' And then this made him be even louder yelling at his daughter than he had been before, and I of course was filled with terror that this was going to get us all thrown in the Big House. I believe the cops thought that we were making porn, and we sent out Nate [Kelly], one of the line producers, who had a little scruffy beard and was wearing a big ill-fitting jacket because we were having him standing in the background as a wedding guest, because we didn't have enough, and I don't think he helped the 'we're not shooting porn' image we were trying to project to the cop there, but then when he came back out, he said, 'Well, this is clearly a big production so I'm shutting you down.' He could have been nicer about it. But he didn't stop us. That's right. [badass accent] We made Shakespeare against the law. We fought Johnny Law for art.

In directing the actors, you and Fran Kranz have both said that you told him to keep in mind that Claudio is a 'temperamental jock.' Were there any other quick descriptions you were able to give other actors?

I would say the only thing that I played that might be accused of playing against the text, but for me just felt completely right emotionally, was the character of Margaret [Ashley Johnson]. Borachio [Spencer Treat Clark] seemed to me to be obsessively in love with Hero. It's the only thing that makes sense to me. He is an unrepentant villain, until after he hears that Hero has died, and then suddenly he's the most repentant villain in the history of villainy. He's actually heroic. And why? [laughs] The only event that made sense for me is him hearing about her death and then you go back and he does mention that he can, at any instant, get Margaret to dress up like Hero in Hero's bedroom. I'm like, 'How often does he do that? That seems like something that's not okay.' [laughs] There's a dark and kind of icky romanticism about him. And then my take on Margaret is, she has to know. You don't dress up like somebody else so that someone will sleep with you and have great self-worth feelings. You don't. That's not going on. She's usually played as sort of a dim and lively bawd, and I feel like there's a great sadness to what she's going through. And when Ashley Johnson played the seduction flashback, she caused an oboe solo. 'We have to put oboe over her on this piece, because she's breaking my heart.' And I see no other reason for Borachio to act the way he does. But I had never seen that interpretation. It's probably occurred, like we said, many times, just not in front of me. But I may have had Margaret playing against the text, particularly in her last scene with Benedick, where she's making a bunch of dirty jokes, but we're playing it like, 'I'm the girl who does *this*, this is what's expected of me.' And then of course having Hero defend her at the end to her father, and [Margaret] actually dancing with her father in the last scene, is her redemptive note. The family loves her; she's back in. And I slightly changed Conrade, I said, 'You should be womanly.'

Why did you decide Conrade should be womanly?
Well, first of all, get more women in the play – nothing wrong with that. Anywhere where gender specificity is not actually an issue in the play, there's no reason not to. And it felt to me like, in a play that's all about relationships, why not play Don John and Conrade as having one? It's a way to make another sly little comment on all of these romances, and it's a way to have more sex.

Also, if Don John is going to have a sexual relationship with one of his minions, if Conrade were male, then the main villain is the only gay character, and it could seem like a correlation was being drawn between villainy and gayness.
Right. 'I despise all people and unions between lovers – I'm the evil gay man!' That didn't feel like that would fly. I toyed with the idea of having Don Pedro be very obviously gay throughout, just so that when Benedick says, 'Get thee a wife,' he could look at Benedick like, 'How dumb are you?'

Don Pedro has quite a flirtatious scene with Beatrice. Is that scene quite so flirtatious in the text?
It's even mentioned later – 'I would have doffed all other aspects and made her half myself.' He says, 'I would totally go there.' And in the Branagh [film version], Denzel

Washington [as Don Pedro] plays that, 'Will you have me, lady?' very sincerely, and it's sweet and it's a little heartbreaking. But when we looked at Don Pedro, we said, 'This guy is playing a game. He's got his buddies and he's coming to party his ass off, because he's just won the day.' And the first thing he does is the most inexplicable thing in the film, which is the, 'I'll tell you what, Claudio. You love Hero – I'm going to dress up like you and pretend that I'm you. That'll help.' That was one we tortured ourselves with. And everybody had a different reason why he might do that. Riki Lindhome, Conrade, she came up with the best one, which was, 'He thinks Claudio will fuck it up. He thinks if Claudio woos her, it's going to go south.' But in the end, we just played it, 'That makes no sense!' And [Don Pedro's] dedication to this very bad idea and Fran's hilarious reaction to it made it work as well as anything in the film, because it is really sort of the kickoff of, 'Let's all start lying and playing games wearing masks, and just ruining everything.' And Don Pedro is extremely likable, but at the same time, definitely the brother of Don John. They are the schemers. And there's a sort of callousness with which he decides to manipulate the lives of the people around him and assumes that he has the right to do that. And he comes down and he's genuinely remorseful that it all goes wrong, but what Reed and I were thinking of with him was that he's not sincerely going to propose to Beatrice, he's in that game. It really is just, he is that party guy, it is a game to him. 'Prince, thou art sad' comes not from, 'Well, I don't have a mate like everybody else.' For us, it came from, 'I just lost my two drinking buddies. And now I've got to go find two more.' And we all felt, 'And within a month, he will. He'll have two other sworn brothers by his side, because this is how he rolls.'

Does Beatrice know that it's Benedick she's talking to at the masked ball?
Yeah, I think so. We played it just dim and dark enough that she could be like, 'It's *probably* him.' The difference that we made there was to have her saying what she said in front of everybody and getting laughs, rather than just saying it to him. When Benedick hits her with 'Harpy,' Alexis was worried that he was being just unlikably fierce, and I'm like, 'Don't forget what she did to you, where she did it,' and then of course, when we shot Amy's side, the look she gave him was so challenging that it justified it. We needed her to bring him up to that rant.

Where did Alexis Denisof come up with that accent in the masked ball scene?
Alexis Denisof is a man of many accents, forty percent of which are completely silly.

Speaking of accents, did you come to the conclusion early on, 'We're going to have all Americans, except for the Friar, who is played by English actor Paul Meston,' or was there ever a thought of, 'Maybe they should do British accents'?
No. You know what? I want people to use their own voices. The thing about

Shakespeare is that he works in any voice. At the readings, we'd do a lot of [roles] in a Southern accent, 'I'm going to go British,' 'I'm going to go super-plummy British.' I definitely did a Feste the Jester pretending to be Father Topas in a silly voice that finally made Tim Minear cry out, 'Where are you from?!' And I was like, 'The Swedish part of Italy.' 'Oh, okay.' But the language, it works because it works. Some people literally think you can't do it without a British accent, and it's nonsense. To have people struggling to add an accent onto the already, 'You have to do eight pages of Elizabethan dialogue every day for twelve days,' that's a bit nuts. That's asking a bit much, and ultimately it comes off as pretentious and phony and false. You're trying to [extreme British received-pronunciation accent] 'do Shakespeare' [regular voice], instead of make a movie.

When Claudio thinks he's being introduced to a stranger he's supposed to marry and says he'll go through with it even if she's 'an Ethiope,' you have an African-American woman right there in frame, reacting to him. How are we supposed to react to Claudio at that moment?

That's sort the culmination of his idiocy. I talked to the woman [Malika Williams] beforehand and I said, 'This is what I want to do.' And before I could say what I meant, how I intended it to play, she said it for me. She said, 'Oh, so it's a Michael Scott moment.' I'm like, 'Yes. We're playing an *Office* gag.' And there's Benedick right behind her, going, 'Oh, Jesus, oh, God, my best friend's such a yutz ...' It felt a little bit risky to keep it, but it just felt also hilarious if you play that everybody in that world is aware of what he just said, except him. I did change Benedick's line, 'If I do not love her, I am a Jew.' There is no way to contextualize that wherein you can say, 'Oh, it's okay, because we're making fun of this, that or the other.' No, that's just not going to play. Whereas the 'Ethiope' thing, Claudio has been so set up to be that guy, it's just taking it into a modern context and poking fun at it.

How was Amy Acker falling down the stairs accomplished? Did you have a mat right below frame-line?

[joking] I just find her to be very expendable. [seriously] We actually had a stunt guy on that day – that was the one day we had a stunt guy there. He built a little platform, we had a mat on it, he was there to spot her, we did everything absolutely as safely as humanly possible, because Amy it turns out is not expendable. Nothing I do is ever worth people breaking themselves for.

With the other physical comedy, how much of that was the actors' suggestions and how much of that was you going, for example, 'Okay, Alexis, now roll over ...'?

Some of the broad strokes and a couple of the specific moves are in the screenplay, or came from our discussions, but a lot of it, and all of the best of it, was Alexis. I

MuchADO ABOUT NOTHING

did indicate that the boys should walk one way and then suddenly reverse direction, because they knew that he was following them, but what he did with that was entirely his own and is priceless. He also came up – on the day – with the entire madman calisthenics that he does when he's decided Beatrice loves him. And I was staring at him going, 'Oh, my God, this is further than I thought we were going to go here.' And it's one of the things that makes audiences applaud.

With Alexis, I gave him the arena and then he used it and then he said, 'Can I have a small branch to hide behind?' And I said, 'Yes, you can.' [laughs] But with Amy everything was a little more specific going in. We worked the gags out together and she was like, 'Can I hit my head more times?' She's fiercely game. But even the score – with Alexis, it's all sort of comedy pizzicato, but it's very all over the place. And with Amy, it's very deliberate – the tune, which is a sneaking-around tune, then goes to, you wouldn't notice it, but it turns into the love theme, which will play really for the first time a minute later, when she's deciding to love Benedick. This deliberateness that I'm describing – one of the things in the movie that mattered the most to me was, you have this very famous scene where Benedick is tricked by his friends. And if done right, it's hilarious. Then you have another scene of the exact same thing [Beatrice being tricked by Hero et al] that's not hilarious, that usually doesn't have the juice that the first one has, because you've seen it. And Beatrice doesn't usually get to play it quite as broadly. For me as a filmmaker, the biggest challenge of the piece was making the second [scene] work on another level from the first one, so that it didn't feel like sloppy seconds, so that it was as delightful and watchable. It's designed visually so that we're with her, she's in the foreground, whereas he was behind the scene. The gags are bigger, like the stair fall. I wanted to go beyond any place we've been, because I wanted this to play as its own scene, and of course, the overacting is – I mean, Emma [Bates as Ursula] is hilarious. Emma and Jillian, their [in-character] bad stiff acting [to get Beatrice to react pushes] her even more slightly over the top, because I just wanted to make sure that I didn't get that feeling that I almost always get from these productions, where it's like, 'Oh, here we go again.'

Some versions of *Much Ado* bring Don John back for a final glare with Don Pedro et al and you opted not to do that …
It just felt like it was a beat I didn't need and the idea that we could see him being manhandled by Verges and Dogberry was a lovely little sendoff for them as well, sort of, 'Hey, once again, the idiots have saved the day.' And I didn't want to do a whole, 'And they enter, and they glare and they pause and they take him away.' This movie needs to be a little more nimble than that.

You have a group of actors who you work with repeatedly, including most of the main cast of *Much Ado*. Do you trust these actors because they trust you so completely?

30

I trust them because they have proved themselves time and again, and they're in my life because I've seen their work and I've spoken with them and they do trust me. That is the only trick I have as a director, is trust. 'You are coming into a safe place where everyone will be treated with respect and where you will be able to go as far as you want, and when it is too far, I will tell you that. And you can trust me. And we will go into the editing room and find your best takes.' People know that they have the room to give everything, and that sometimes everything is too much. And without them, I'm nothing, I'm making dead-eyed mo-cap. This whole venture only works because I have these extraordinary people in my life and if they don't trust me, they're doing a very good job of hiding it.

Tom Lenk once said, 'If Joss Whedon asked me to do performance art in a water fountain, I'd do it.'
Tom was already doing that.

When and why did you decide that you were going to write the film's musical score? Did you feel like you didn't have enough to do?
Yeah, I have a problem. You know, originally, I wanted Jed [Whedon] to do it, but he just didn't have time, and the money we were offering him was not even plural. So at some point, I just went, 'I desperately want to do this, and nobody else is ever going to hire me to do it, and we don't have a release date. So I'm just going to go for it.' It was hard, I was terrified and not conversant with the [computer] program Pro Logic, and I took a lot of hand-holding and [producer Danny] Kaminsky, who was running all of post, did eventually have to say, 'Joss, I know you're under a lot of pressure right now, but every day we don't finish post, it's costing us money, and will you please write the score?' Then, when we brought in [music score producer] Debbie Lurie, an orchestrator, and she listened to some of the cues, she was like, 'Oh, this is good.' The next morning, I wrote an entire reel in three hours. [laughs] I just needed somebody to tell me, 'You are not insane.' But first of all, what fun for me. Second of all, if we're not learning, then why are we working? And third, I knew what I wanted – I didn't know what it sounded like, but I knew what it was, and that's an exciting challenge to give yourself as a composer, to say, 'I have this feeling of a romantic but noir comedy and how am I going to express that?' There are so many different ways you can go. At the end, I'm not that facile with instruments. I just sort of followed my fingers and certain things began to make sense and then I learned so much in the process about – not that I got it all right, but when to come in, when to stay out, what tools [to use]. I found out that layering three different moods in the space of forty seconds is actually much easier than sustaining one for two minutes. Being the composer is playing a part. Learning that, the way you can only really learn it, by doing it, was dazzling.

What did you write the score on?

It's Pro Logic and I've got a keyboard attached to a computer, and then I can sample instruments from that, and then I can play. In some cases, it's very specific; in some cases, I would just sort of riff and then Debbie would pick a melody out of this mélange of junk I'd given her for the cues. But I'd worked out my basic themes – love theme, Hero's theme, the main theme, villian theme, Borachio – and then everything I did became a variation or combination on those, pretty much. And so it was all done on piano, but the sampling is extraordinary, so you can orchestrate really effectively even while sketching. And then of course it was my party, so I decided we would record instruments live. We don't have a ton – it is not the London Symphony Orchestra, but we did get live music in there, which felt right. I didn't want to do a synthetic score.

What Shakespeare do you think you'll do next and what need to be the circumstances allowing you to do it?

Twelfth Night and *Hamlet* are the two favorites of mine. And circumstance, we need a lot of time, more than twelve days, and everything would have to come together. Would I be able to cast these things? *Hamlet*'s a toughie, because it's very much an ensemble play, but boy, you've got to get that part right. And every actor becomes the reason you're doing that production – you can't slot somebody in and so it's tough, because your idea about what the movie is is going to change, based on who you cast. But the only thing I don't have is time, of course. This was also something I had never done, and now it's not. This isn't the BBC, just filming all of the [Shakespeare] canon – although that sounds fun, don't get me wrong. If I made another movie, it would be because there was [a reason to make] another movie, not just because it's fun for me.

You've said you found making *Much Ado About Nothing* therapeutic. Can you elaborate on that?

Well, I've never been happier. Those readings were a source of enormous joy for me. Some pressure – I was basically producing in my spare time from producing. But to have that shot of just pure excitement and joy sustained for twelve whole days, to know that it was going to live on, to know that I wasn't just listening to the beautiful words that my talented friends were saying, but I was actually getting to be a part of it the whole time as the director, interpreting the words. It's the first Shakespeare I've ever directed – as I said, I've never done any theatre. And getting to be at that party and not just because it was at my house – it was a perfect storm of the things I love, and out of it came art. And either of those things makes life worth living. Both together is beyond a privilege.

38

MUCH ADO ABOUT NOTHING

DRAMATIS PERSONAE

Amy Acker
BEATRICE
Niece to Leonato

Alexis Denisof
BENEDICK
a young Lord of Padua

Reed Diamond
DON PEDRO
Prince of Arragon

Sean Maher
DON JOHN
his bastard brother

Clark Gregg
LEONATO
Governor of Messina

Fran Kranz
CLAUDIO
a young Lord of Florence

Jillian Morgese
HERO
Daughter to Leonato

Nathan Fillion
DOGBERRY
a Constable

Tom Lenk
VERGES
a Headborough

Spencer Treat Clark
BORACHIO
Follower of Don John

Riki Lindhome
CONRADE
Follower of Don John

Paul M. Meston
FRIAR FRANCIS

Ashley Johnson
MARGARET
Gentlewoman attending Hero

Emma Bates
URSULA
Gentlewoman attending Hero.

Joshua Zar
AIDE TO LEONATO

Romy Rosemont
THE SEXTON

Elsa Guillet-Chapuis
THE COURT PHOTOGRAPHER

MUCH ADO ABOUT NOTHING

THE SCREENPLAY

INT. APARTMENT BEDROOM - MORNING INT. APARTMENT
BEDROOM - MORNING

*We see the classic day-after tableau: there's been a party, there's been
a more private party. BEATRICE lies in bed as BENEDICK quietly
dresses. Neither of them says anything. He approaches her and she
fakes sleep. He hesitates, then grabs his tie and exits.*

EXT. STREET - DAY

It is a beautiful, sun-dappled street, lined with enormous old trees.

TITLE: MUCH ADO ABOUT NOTHING

*From behind one tree steps a WATCHMAN, a sort of detective,
speaking into the com in his sleeve. Another appears from behind
another tree several yards away in a similar grey suit.*

ANGLE: Through the street drive a few black sedans, in slow state.

INT. LEONATO'S ESTATE, KITCHEN - DAY

*The kitchen is abustle with people preparing food and elaborate
punches, among them Beatrice (a few years older than we saw before)
and HERO, her cousin, both working but neither clearly members of
the household staff (who wear aprons). Beatrice wields a cutting knife,
slicing oranges for a sangria.*

*LEONATO enters with Balthus, his ever-present AIDE. Leonato reads
from an iphone...*

LEONATO

I learn in this letter that Don Pedro of Aragon comes
this day to Messina.

AIDE

He is very near by this: not three leagues off.

LEONATO

How many gentlemen have been lost in this action?

AIDE

But few of any sort, and none of name.

LEONATO

(to Hero)

A victory is twice itself when the achiever brings home
full numbers. I find here that Don Pedro hath bestowed
much honour on a young Florentine called Claudio.

AIDE

Much deserved on his part and equally remembered
by Don Pedro: he hath borne himself beyond the
promise of his age, doing, in the figure of a lamb, the
feats of a lion.

She blushes, pleased and awkward simultaneously.

BEATRICE

I pray you, is Signior Mountanto returned from the
wars or no?

AIDE

I know none of that name, lady.

HERO

(pulling a tray from the oven)

My cousin means Signior Benedick of Padua.

AIDE

O, he's returned; and as pleasant as ever he was.

BEATRICE

I pray you, how many hath he killed and eaten in
these wars? But how many hath he killed? For indeed I
promised to eat all of his killing.

LEONATO

(signing papers)

Faith, niece, you tax Signior Benedick too much; but
he'll be meet with you, I doubt it not.

AIDE

He hath done good service, lady, in these wars.

BEATRICE

You had musty victual, and he hath holp to eat it: he is a
very valiant trencherman; he hath an excellent stomach.

AIDE

And a good soldier too, lady.

BEATRICE

And a good soldier to a lady: but what is he to a lord?

AIDE

A lord to a lord, a man to a man; stuffed with all honourable virtues.

BEATRICE

It is so, indeed; he is no less than a stuffed man: but for the stuffing,-- well, we are all mortal.

LEONATO

You must not, sir, mistake my niece. There is a kind of merry war betwixt Signior Benedick and her -

She mouths "merry?", looking at him peevishly. Only Hero sees.

LEONATO (CONT'D)

-- they never meet but there's a skirmish of wit between them.

BEATRICE

Who is his companion now? He hath every month a new sworn brother.

AIDE

Is't possible?

BEATRICE

Very easily possible: he wears his faith but as the
fashion of his hat; it ever changes with the next block.

AIDE

I see, lady, the gentleman is not in your books.

BEATRICE

No; an he were, I would burn my study. But, I pray you,
who is his companion? Is there no young squarer now
that will make a voyage with him to the devil?

AIDE

He is most in the company of the right noble Claudio.

BEATRICE

O Lord, he will hang upon him like a disease: he is
sooner caught than the pestilence, and the taker
runs presently mad. God help the noble Claudio! if he
have caught the Benedick, it will cost him a thousand
pound ere a' be cured.

EXT. LEONATO'S ESTATE, FRONT YARD - DAY

*The three cars pull up. VERGES and two other watchmen position
themselves by the last car.*

*DON PEDRO emerges from the first car, CLAUDIO and
BENEDICK(now bearded) from the second. From the last, DON JOHN,
his girlfriend CONRADE, and his protégé BORACHIO all emerge,
their hands bound. Don Pedro sees this and frowns, indicates to the
watchman to free them, which he does as Leonato and a few of his*

retinue emerge from the gate. Among them is a PHOTOGRAPHER, who is constantly about the estate, snapping candids.

DON PEDRO

Good Signior Leonato, you are come to meet your trouble: the fashion of the world is to avoid cost, and you encounter it.

LEONATO

(hugs him)

Never came trouble to my house in the likeness of your grace...

They pose for the official photo, real warmth replaced with stately smiles, as the others approach, Benedick and Claudio in front.

LEONATO (CONT'D)

...for trouble being gone, comfort should remain, but when you depart from me, sorrow abides and happiness takes his leave.

DON PEDRO

You embrace your charge too willingly. I think this is your daughter.

Hero is emerging from the gate, trying not to appear as though she's seeking out Claudio.

ANGLE: CLAUDIO is stunned by her.

ANGLE: BORACHIO, darkly, stares at her also.

LEONATO
Her mother hath many times told me so.

BENEDICK
Were you in doubt, sir, that you asked her?

LEONATO
Signior Benedick, no; for then were you a child.

DON PEDRO
Truly, the lady fathers herself. Be happy, lady; for you
are like an honourable father.

*As everyone greets each other -- Claudio suddenly nervous with Hero,
and Margaret waving covertly to an unresponsive Borachio -- Benedick
continues, circling near the entrance to the courtyard.*

BENEDICK
If Signior Leonato be her father, she would not have
his head on her shoulders for all Messina, as like him
as she is.

BEATRICE
(appearing behind him)
I wonder that you will still be talking, Signior
Benedick: nobody marks you.

EXT. COURTYARD - DAY

He turns and enters the courtyard as she backs away, putting out the flowers she has brought to arrange. He follows, absently upsetting her arrangements.

BENEDICK

What, my dear Lady Disdain! Are you yet living?

BEATRICE

Is it possible disdain should die while she hath such meet food to feed it as Signior Benedick? Courtesy itself must convert to disdain, if you come in her presence.

BENEDICK

Then is courtesy a turncoat. But it is certain I am loved of all ladies, only you excepted: and I would I could find in my heart that I had not a hard heart; for, truly, I love none.

BEATRICE

A dear happiness to women: they would else have been troubled with a pernicious suitor. I thank God and my cold blood, I am of your humour for that: I had rather hear my dog bark at a crow than a man swear he loves me.

BENEDICK

God keep your ladyship still in that mind! So some gentleman or other shall 'scape a predestinate scratched face.

BEATRICE

Scratching could not make it worse, an 'twere such a
face as yours were.

BENEDICK

Well, you are a rare parrot-teacher.

BEATRICE

A bird of my tongue is better than a beast of yours.

BENEDICK

I would my horse had the speed of your tongue, and so
good a continuer. But keep your way, i' God's name; I
have done.

BEATRICE

You always end with a jade's trick: I know you of old.

They're staring at each other as the others pour in through the gate.

DON PEDRO

Signior Benedick, my dear friend Leonato hath invited
you all.
I tell him we shall stay here at the least a month; and
he heartily prays some occasion may detain us longer.

LEONATO
(To DON JOHN)

Let me bid you welcome, my lord: being reconciled to
the prince your brother, I owe you all duty.

DON JOHN

I thank you: I am not of many words, but I thank you.

LEONATO

Please it your grace lead on?

DON PEDRO

Your hand, Leonato; we will go together.

They start in. The photographer snapping a candid of Don John looking after them. Looking not so reconciled.

INT. UPSTAIRS/BENEDICK'S ROOM - DAY

Benedick and Claudio carry their suitcases up, seeking out their room.

CLAUDIO

Benedick, didst thou note the daughter of Signior Leonato?

BENEDICK

I noted her not; but I looked on her.

CLAUDIO

Is she not a modest young lady?

BENEDICK

Do you question me, as an honest man should do, for my simple true judgment; or would you have me

speak after my custom, as being a professed tyrant to
their sex?

CLAUDIO
No; I pray thee speak in sober judgment.

*Benedick enters the little pink room with twin beds, looking sourly at
the unicorny decor.*

BENEDICK
Why, i' faith, methinks she's too low for a high praise,
too brown for a fair praise and too little for a great
praise: only this commendation I can afford her, that
were she other than she is, she were unhandsome;
and being no other but as she is, I do not like her.

CLAUDIO
Thou thinkest I am in sport: I pray thee tell me truly
how thou likest her.

BENEDICK
Would you buy her, that you inquire after her?

CLAUDIO
(moves back to the stairs)
Can the world buy such a jewel?

BENEDICK
Yea, and a case to put it into. But speak you this with a
sad brow?

CLAUDIO

In mine eye she is the sweetest lady that ever I looked on.

ANGLE: from his POV, we see Hero and Beatrice, still arranging flowers.

BENEDICK

(looks down as well)

I can see yet without spectacles and I see no such matter: there's her cousin, an she were not possessed with a fury, exceeds her as much in beauty as the first of May doth the last of December. But I hope you have no intent to turn husband, have you?

They head back into their room.

CLAUDIO

I would scarce trust myself, though I had sworn the contrary, if Hero would be my wife.

Benedick drops into a chair right next to an enormous doll-house.

BENEDICK

Is't come to this? Shall I never see a bachelor of three-score again? Go to, i' faith; an thou wilt needs thrust thy neck into a yoke, wear the print of it and sigh away Sundays.

Don Pedro sticks his head in from an adjoining bathroom.

DON PEDRO

What secret hath held you here, that you followed not Leonato?

BENEDICK

I would your grace would constrain me to tell.

DON PEDRO

I charge thee on thy allegiance.

Claudio tries to stop Benedick, but:

BENEDICK

You hear, Count Claudio: on my allegiance, mark you this, on my allegiance.
(to Don Pedro)
He is in love. With who? Now that is your grace's part. Mark how short his answer is -- With Hero, Leonato's short daughter.

DON PEDRO

Amen, if you love her; for the lady is very well worthy.

CLAUDIO

You speak this to fetch me in, my lord.

DON PEDRO

By my troth, I speak my thought.

CLAUDIO

And, in faith, my lord, I spoke mine.

BENEDICK

And, by my two faiths and troths, my lord, I spoke mine.

CLAUDIO

That I love her, I feel.

DON PEDRO

That she is worthy, I know.

BENEDICK

(entering the closet)

That I neither feel how she should be loved nor know how she should be worthy, is the opinion that fire cannot melt out of me: I will die in it at the stake.

DON PEDRO

Thou wast ever an obstinate heretic in the despite of beauty.

BENEDICK

(emerges, holding up frilly girl-clothes)

That a woman conceived me, I thank her; that she brought me up, I likewise give her most humble

thanks: but that I will have a recheat winded in my
forehead, or hang my bugle in an invisible baldrick,
all women shall pardon me. Because I will not do them
the wrong to mistrust any, I will do myself the right to
trust none; and the fine is, for the which I may go the
finer, I will live a bachelor.

DON PEDRO

I shall see thee, ere I die, look pale with love.

BENEDICK

With anger, with sickness, or with hunger, my lord,
not with love.

DON PEDRO

Well, as time shall try: 'In time the savage bull doth
bear the yoke.'

BENEDICK

The savage bull may; but if ever the sensible Benedick
bear it, pluck off the bull's horns and set them in my
forehead: and let me be vilely painted, and in such
great letters as they write 'Here is good horse to hire,'
let them signify under my sign, 'Here you may see
Benedick the married man.'

DON PEDRO

Nay, if Cupid have not spent all his quiver in Venice,
thou wilt quake for this shortly.

BENEDICK

I look for an earthquake too, then.

Don Pedro exits to his own room, Claudio following.

INT. DON PEDRO'S ROOM - DAY

It's the boy version of the other, but with one big bed.

CLAUDIO

Hath Leonato any son, my lord?

DON PEDRO

No child but Hero; she's his only heir. Dost thou affect
her, Claudio?

CLAUDIO

O, my lord, When you went onward on this ended
action, I look'd upon her with a soldier's eye, That
liked, but had a rougher task in hand than to drive
liking to the name of love: But now I am return'd and
that war-thoughts have left their places vacant, in
their rooms Come thronging soft and delicate desires,
all prompting me how fair young Hero is, saying, I
liked her ere I went to wars.

DON PEDRO

Thou wilt be like a lover presently And tire the
hearer with a book of words. If thou dost love fair
Hero, cherish it, And I will break with her and with
her father, And thou shalt have her. I know we shall

have revelling to-night: I will assume thy part in some
disguise and tell fair Hero I am Claudio, and in her
bosom I'll unclasp my heart and take her hearing
prisoner with the force and strong encounter of my
amorous tale: Then after to her father will I break;
And the conclusion is, she shall be thine.

*ANGLE: BENEDICK has wandered in, grumpily assessing Don Pedro's
less girly quarters.*

INT. DON JOHN'S BEDROOM -DAY

*Don John lies in bed in his shirtsleeves, Conrade wrapped around him,
head on his chest. He stares.*

> CONRADE
What the good-year, my lord! Why are you thus out of
measure sad?

> DON JOHN
There is no measure in the occasion that breeds;
therefore the sadness is without limit.

> CONRADE
You should hear reason.

> DON JOHN
And when I have heard it, what blessing brings it?

CONRADE

If not a present remedy, at least a patient sufferance.
He moves off the bed, looking up out the french door:
to see an agent standing guard on the stairs above.

DON JOHN

I cannot hide what I am: I must be sad when I have
cause and smile at no man's jests, eat when I have
stomach and wait for no man's leisure, sleep when
I am drowsy and tend on no man's business, laugh
when I am merry and claw no man in his humour.

CONRADE

Yea, but you must not make the full show of this till
you may do it without controlment. You have of late
stood out against your brother, and he hath ta'en you
newly into his grace; where it is impossible you should
take true root but by the fair weather that you make
yourself.

As she speaks he moves back to the bed, popping a button at the
bottom of her blouse and kissing her belly. Working his way up:

DON JOHN

I had rather be a canker in a hedge than a rose in his
grace, and it better fits my blood to be disdained of all
than to fashion a carriage to rob love from any: in this,
though I cannot be said to be a flattering honest man,
it must not be denied but I am a plain-dealing villain.
I am trusted with a muzzle and enfranchised with a
clog. If I had my mouth --
                    (kisses her deeply)
-- I would bite.

It's getting heavy between them.

> CONRADE
> (suggestively)
> Can you make no use of your discontent?

> DON JOHN
> I make all use of it, for I use it only.

They go at each other savagely -- and Borachio enters, a bit drunk. Don John stops, shifting gears, as Conrade grits her teeth and throws the sheet over her lower half.

> DON JOHN (CONT'D)
> What news, Borachio?

> BORACHIO
> I came yonder from a great supper: the prince your brother is royally entertained by Leonato: and I can give you intelligence of an intended marriage.

Don John slips his hand under the sheet, caressing Conrade as he questions Borachio.

> DON JOHN
> Will it serve for any model to build mischief on? What is he for a fool that betroths himself to unquietness?

BORACHIO

Marry, it is your brother's right hand.

DON JOHN

Who? The most exquisite Claudio?

BORACHIO

Even he.

DON JOHN

A proper squire! And who, and who? Which way looks
he?

BORACHIO
(desolate)
Marry, on Hero, the daughter and heir of Leonato.

DON JOHN

A very forward March-chick!

BORACHIO

I heard it agreed upon that the prince should woo
Hero for himself, and having obtained her, give her to
Count Claudio.

DON JOHN
(standing)
Come, come, let us thither: this may prove food to my
displeasure. That young start-up hath all the glory
of my overthrow: if I can cross him any way, I bless

myself every way. You are both sure, and will assist
me?

*Borachio is out the door, but Conrade closes it behind him, turning to
Don John.*

CONRADE
To the death, my lord.

She smiles, kissing him hard.

INT. DINING ROOM - NIGHT

*Servants are clearing up as Leonato, Hero and Beatrice sit with after-
dinner drinks.*

LEONATO
Was not Count John here at supper?

HERO
I saw him not.

BEATRICE
How tartly that gentleman looks! I never can see him
but I am heart-burned an hour after.

HERO
He is of a very melancholy disposition.

BEATRICE

He were an excellent man that were made just in the
midway between him and Benedick: the one is too like
an image and says nothing, and the other too like my
lady's eldest son, evermore tattling.

LEONATO

By my troth, niece, thou wilt never get thee a husband,
if thou be so shrewd of thy tongue.

*URSULA brings in a box of costumes and masks. The three of them
rise, Hero first, to choose. As she holds up various manly masks...*

BEATRICE

For the which blessing I am upon my knees every
morning and evening. Lord, I could not endure a
husband with a beard on his face: I had rather lie in
the woollen.

LEONATO

You may light on a husband that hath no beard.

*He tries on a mask -- and his Aide is there with a mirror to show him
how it looks. He tries another.*

BEATRICE

What should I do with him?
                    (holding a mask to Ursula's face)
dress him in my apparel and make him my waiting-
gentlewoman? He that hath a beard is more than a
youth, and he that hath no beard is less than a man:

and he that is more than a youth is not for me, and he
that is less than a man, I am not for him: therefore.

LEONATO

[To HERO] I trust you will be ruled by your father.

BEATRICE

Yes, faith; it is my cousin's duty to make curtsy and say
'Father, as it please you.' But yet for all that, cousin,
let him be a handsome fellow, or else make another
curtsy and say 'Father, as it please me.'

LEONATO
(leading Hero out)
Well, niece, I hope to see you one day fitted with a
husband.

BEATRICE

Not till God make men of some other metal
than earth. Would it not grieve a woman to be
overmastered with a piece of valiant dust? To make an
account of her life to a clod of wayward marl?

She realizes she is alone.

EXT. BACKYARD - NIGHT

*Where the party is starting. Formal, but decently raucous, with various
masks and get-ups peppering the suits and gowns. Don Pedro sees Hero
with Beatrice, and pulling down his mask, approaches her.*

DON PEDRO
Lady, will you walk about with your friend?

She takes his arm and they go off together. Beatrice watches, not entirely approving.

EXT. BACKYARD - LATER

MUSIC ("Sigh No More") OVER:

EXT. BACKYARD - NIGHT

A bartender serves drinks. Claudio is surrounded by young men urging him to down a drink, frat-boy style...

EXT. POOL - NIGHT

People dive in, play about. Some with undies and shirts instead of suits, most with drinks.

EXT. BACKYARD - NIGHT

On a trapeze, twin sisters perform an intricate, sensuous act...

INT. BACKYARD - NIGHT

A couple sneaks down past the back gate with amorous intent.

INT. DINING ROOM - NIGHT

People stand around the piano, where for a moment the song playing over the party goes live -- just a woman singing and a man at the keys.

EXT. BACKYARD - NIGHT

A group are dancing off to one side. Margaret watches Borachio among the crowd, trying to get his attention as she fends off the attentions of Leonato's Aide.

> AIDE
> Well, I would you did like me.

> MARGARET
> So would not I, for your own sake; for I have many ill-qualities.

> AIDE
> Which is one?

> MARGARET
> I say my prayers aloud.

> AIDE
> I love you the better: the hearers may cry, Amen.

MARGARET
(eyes on Borachio)
God match me with a good dancer...

EXT. BACKYARD FIRE PIT - NIGHT

ANGLE: BEATRICE AND BENEDICK are by the fire pit. She sits among friends on the couch, occasionally fending off the wayward hands of a drunk fellow. Benedick is nearer the pit, more in shadow, toasting a marshmallow.

BEATRICE
Will you not tell me who told you so?

BENEDICK
No, you shall pardon me.

BEATRICE
Nor will you not tell me who you are?

BENEDICK
Not now.

Ursula sits and Beatrice brings her up to speed:

BEATRICE
That I was disdainful, and that I had my good wit out
of the 'Hundred Merry Tales:'-- well this was Signior
Benedick that said so.

BENEDICK

What's he?

BEATRICE

I am sure you know him well enough.

BENEDICK

Not I, believe me.

BEATRICE

Did he never make you laugh?

BENEDICK

I pray you, what is he?

BEATRICE

Why, he is the prince's jester: a very dull fool; only
his gift is in devising impossible slanders: none but
libertines delight in him; and the commendation is
not in his wit, but in his villany; for he both pleases
men and angers them, and then they laugh at him and
beat him.

*Benedick raises a flaming marshmallow into frame, glowering. He
drops it as Beatrice pushes away the drunk fellow once and for all.*

BEATRICE (CONT'D)

I am sure he is in the fleet: I would he had boarded
me.

BENEDICK
When I know the gentleman, I'll tell him what you say.

A conga line forms nearby.

BEATRICE
Do, do: he'll but break a comparison or two on me;
which, peradventure not marked or not laughed
at, strikes him into melancholy; and then there's a
partridge wing saved, for the fool will eat no supper
that night.

She makes her way toward the line, Drunk Guy following.

BEATRICE (CONT'D)
We must follow the leaders.

*Benedick gets between Beatrice and Drunk Guy, holding her a bit too
low.*

BENEDICK
In every good thing.

BEATRICE
(slapping away his hand)
Nay, if they lead to any ill, I will leave them at the next
turning.

Drunk Guy falls in behind Benedick, grabbing HIM a bit too low.

EXT. POOL - SUNRISE

A girl is passed out on the couch nearby. Claudio is in the pool, wearing a mask and snorkle, drinking. Don John, Borachio and Conrade all swim up behind him.

DON JOHN
Are not you Signior Benedick?

CLAUDIO
You know me well; I am he.

DON JOHN
Signior, you are very near my brother in his love: he is enamoured on Hero; I pray you, dissuade him from her: she is no equal for his birth: you may do the part of an honest man in it.

CLAUDIO
How know you he loves her?

DON JOHN
I heard him swear his affection.

BORACHIO
So did I too; and he swore he would marry her to-night.

DON JOHN
Come, let us to the banquet.

Exeunt, swimming away. Claudio pulls off his mask, gets out.

CLAUDIO
'Tis certain so; the prince wooes for himself.
Friendship is constant in all other things
Save in the office and affairs of love: for beauty is a
witch Against whose charms faith melteth into blood.

He's toweling off as Benedick approaches.

BENEDICK
Count Claudio?

CLAUDIO
Yea, the same.

BENEDICK
Come, will you go with me? The prince hath got your
Hero.

CLAUDIO
I wish him joy of her.

BENEDICK
Did you think the prince would have served you thus?

CLAUDIO
I pray you, leave me.

BENEDICK

Ho! Now you strike like the blind man: 'twas the boy
that stole your meat, and you'll beat the post.

CLAUDIO

If it will not be, I'll leave you.

Claudio stalks off.

BENEDICK

Alas, poor hurt fowl! Now will he creep into sedges.
But that my Lady Beatrice should know me, and not
know me! The prince's fool! Ha? It may be I go under
that title because I am merry. Yea, but so I am apt to
do myself wrong; I am not so reputed: it is the base,
though bitter, disposition of Beatrice that puts the
world into her person and so gives me out. Well, I'll be
revenged as I may.

INT. KITCHEN - EARLY MORNING

*Benedick enters to find Hero and Don Pedro gathered about the island,
Hero picking at the last of the food and Don Pedro plucking at a guitar.
Leonato is in the breakfast nook, sleeping in his chair. Shots have been
done here, most of them by Don Pedro.*

DON PEDRO

Now, signior, where's the count? did you see him?

BENEDICK

Troth, my lord, I found him as melancholy as a lodge

in a warren: I told him, and I think I told him true,
that your grace had got the good will of this young
lady.

Don Pedro smiles affectionately -- then scowls suddenly.

DON PEDRO

The Lady Beatrice hath a quarrel to you: the
gentleman that danced with her told her she is much
wronged by you.

BENEDICK

O, she misused me past the endurance of a block!
She told me, not thinking I had been myself, that I
was the prince's jester, that I was duller than a great
thaw; huddling jest upon jest with such impossible
conveyance upon me that I stood like a man at a
mark, with a whole army shooting at me. She speaks
poniards, and every word stabs: if her breath were as
terrible as her terminations, there were no living near
her; she would infect to the north star. I would not
marry her --

Don Pedro reacts to the word "marry" having come out of nowhere...

BENEDICK (CONT'D)

-- though she were endowed with all that Adam bad
left him before he transgressed. Come, talk not of her.
I would to God some scholar would conjure her; for
certainly, while she is here, all disquiet, horror and
perturbation follows her.

DON PEDRO

Look, here she comes.

Beatrice enters with a sullen Claudio (now dressed again, hair still wet), stopping to hear:

BENEDICK

Will your grace command me any service to the world's end? I will go on the slightest errand now to the Antipodes that you can devise to send me on; I will fetch you a tooth-picker now from the furthest inch of Asia, bring you a hair off the great Cham's beard, do you any embassage to the Pigmies, rather than hold three words' conference with this harpy. You have no employment for me?

DON PEDRO

None, but to desire your good company.

BENEDICK

O God, sir, here's a dish I love not: I cannot endure my Lady Tongue.

Benedick exits. Beatrice has slipped from amusement to cold silence.

DON PEDRO

Come, lady, come; you have lost the heart of Signior Benedick.

BEATRICE
(truthfully)
Indeed, my lord, he lent it me awhile; and I gave him
use for it, a double heart for his single one.

INT. APARTMENT BEDROOM - NIGHT

*A quick flash of Beatrice from years ago, smiling as Benedick nuzzles
her neck from behind, slipping her dress from her shoulder*

INT. KITCHEN - MORNING

She starts out of the reverie, putting on a smile.

BEATRICE
-- marry, once before he won it of me with false dice,
therefore your grace may well say I have lost it.

DON PEDRO
You have put him down, lady, you have put him down.

BEATRICE
So I would not he should do me, my lord, lest I should
prove the mother of fools. I have brought Count
Claudio, whom you sent me to seek.

DON PEDRO
Why, how now, count! Wherefore are you sad?

CLAUDIO

Not sad, my lord.

DON PEDRO

How then? Sick?

CLAUDIO

Neither, my lord.

BEATRICE

The count is neither sad, nor sick, nor merry, nor well;
but civil count, civil as an orange, and something of
that jealous complexion.

DON PEDRO

I' faith, lady, I think your blazon to be true; though,
I'll be sworn, if he be so, his conceit is false. Here,
Claudio, I have wooed in thy name, and fair Hero is
won: I have broke with her father, and his good will
obtained: name the day of marriage, and God give
thee joy!

*Hero moves to her father and nudges him. He wakes and instantly
begins:*

LEONATO

Count, take of me my daughter, and with her my
fortunes: his grace hath made the match, and all grace
say Amen to it.

BEATRICE

Speak, count, 'tis your cue.

CLAUDIO

Silence is the perfectest herald of joy: I were but little
happy, if I could say how much. Lady, as you are mine,
I am yours: I give away myself for you and dote upon
the exchange.

BEATRICE

Speak, cousin; or, if you cannot, stop his mouth with a
kiss, and let not him speak neither.

DON PEDRO

In faith, lady, you have a merry heart.

BEATRICE

Yea, my lord; I thank it, poor fool, it keeps on the
windy side of care. My cousin tells him in his ear that
he is in her heart.

CLAUDIO

And so she doth, cousin.

BEATRICE

Good Lord, for alliance! Thus goes every one to the
world but I, and I am sunburnt; I may sit in a corner
and cry heigh-ho for a husband!

DON PEDRO
(putting aside his guitar)
Lady Beatrice, I will get you one.

BEATRICE
I would rather have one of your father's getting. Hath
your grace ne'er a brother like you? Your father got
excellent husbands, if a maid could come by them.

DON PEDRO
Will you have me, lady?

He goes down on one knee - and nearly topples. Beatrice helps him up...

BEATRICE
No, my lord, unless I might have another for working-
days: your grace is too costly to wear every day. But, I
beseech your grace, pardon me: I was born to speak all
mirth and no matter.

DON PEDRO
Your silence most offends me, and to be merry best
becomes you; for, out of question, you were born in a
merry hour.

BEATRICE
No, sure, my lord, my mother cried; but then there
was a star danced, and under that was I born. Cousins,
God give you joy!

Beatrice exits.

DON PEDRO
By my troth, a pleasant-spirited lady.

LEONATO
There's little of the melancholy element in her, my
lord: she is never sad but when she sleeps, and not
ever sad then; for I have heard my daughter say, she
hath often dreamed of unhappiness and waked herself
with laughing.

DON PEDRO
She cannot endure to hear tell of a husband.

LEONATO
O, by no means: she mocks all her wooers out of suit.

DON PEDRO
She were an excellent wife for Benedict.

LEONATO
(horrified)
O Lord, my lord, if they were but a week married, they
would talk themselves mad.

DON PEDRO
County Claudio, when mean you to go to church?

CLAUDIO

To-morrow, my lord: time goes on crutches till love
have all his rites.

LEONATO

Not till Monday, my dear son, which is hence a just
seven-night; and a time too brief, too, to have all
things answer my mind.

DON PEDRO

I warrant thee, Claudio, the time shall not go dully by
us. I will in the interim undertake one of Hercules'
labours; which is, to bring Signior Benedick and the
Lady
Beatrice into a mountain of affection the one with the
other. I would fain have it a match, and I doubt not
but to fashion it, if you three will minister assistance.

LEONATO

My lord, I am for you, though it cost me ten nights'
watchings.

CLAUDIO

And I, my lord.

DON PEDRO

And you too, gentle Hero?

HERO

I will do any modest office, my lord, to help my cousin
to a good husband.

Don Pedro starts pouring out a round of shots.

DON PEDRO

And Benedick is not the unhopefullest husband that
I know. Thus far can I praise him; he is of a noble
strain, of approved valour and confirmed honesty. I
will teach you how to humour your cousin, that she
shall fall in love with Benedick; and I, with your two
helps, will so practise on Benedick that, in despite
of his quick wit and his queasy stomach, he shall fall
in love with Beatrice. If we can do this, Cupid is no
longer an archer:
his glory shall be ours --
                         (raising his glass)
--for we are the only love-gods.

They down their shots and slam them on the counter.

ANGLE: THROUGH THE SMALL WINDOW AT THE STAIR we see
them pouring another. PULL BACK to reveal they are being watched by
Don John.

INT. UPSTAIRS/HALLWAY - MORNING

He turns to Borachio, who stands at the head of the stairs.

DON JOHN

It is so; the Count Claudio shall marry the daughter of
Leonato.

BORACHIO

Yea, my lord; but I can cross it.

He starts toward him, and they move quietly through
the hall.

DON JOHN

Any bar, any cross, any impediment will be
medicinable to me: I am sick in displeasure to him,
and whatsoever comes athwart his affection ranges
evenly with mine. How canst thou cross this marriage?

*Margaret crosses from Hero's bedroom, marching an amorous couple
to their own room. Borachio indicates her.*

BORACHIO

I think I told your lordship a year since, how
much I am in the favour of Margaret, the waiting
gentlewoman to Hero.

DON JOHN

I remember.

BORACHIO

I can, at any unseasonable instant of the night,
appoint her to look out at her lady's chamber window.

They look into:

INT. HERO'S BEDROOM - MORNING

DON JOHN
What life is in that, to be the death of this marriage?

Borachio enters the room like it's a holy place, hypnotized by the sight of Hero's bed.

BORACHIO
The poison of that lies in you to temper. Go you to
the prince your brother; spare not to tell him that he
hath wronged his honour in marrying the renowned
Claudio-whose estimation do you mightily hold up --
to a contaminated stale, such a one as Hero.

He takes up her picture as he says it, staring.

DON JOHN
What proof shall I make of that?

BORACHIO
Proof enough to misuse the prince, to vex Claudio, to
undo Hero and kill Leonato.
                    (turning to Don John)
Look you for any other issue?

Don John smiles.

EXT. LOWER WOODS - DAY

Benedick is in workout clothes, running up the stairs toward the house. He sees wedding prep, and turns to see:

ANGLE: FRIAR FRANCIS is in the amphitheater, rehearsing with Hero and Beatrice.

Benedick starts back down.

> BENEDICK
>
> I do much wonder that one man, seeing how much another man is a fool when he dedicates his behaviors to love, will, after he hath laughed at such shallow follies in others, become the argument of his own scorn by failing in love: and such a man is Claudio. I have known when there was no music with him but the drum and the fife; and now had he rather hear the tabour and the pipe: I have known when he would have walked ten mile a-foot to see a good armour; and now will he lie ten nights awake, carving the fashion of a new doublet. He was wont to speak plain and to the purpose, like an honest man and a soldier; and now is he turned orthography; his words are a very fantastical banquet, just so many strange dishes. May I be so converted and see with these eyes? I cannot tell; I think not: I will not be sworn, but love may transform me to an oyster; but I'll take my oath on it, till he have made an oyster of me, he shall never make me such a fool.

Two female servants pass by, smiling at him...

BENEDICK (CONT'D)

One woman is fair, yet I am well; another is wise, yet
I am well; another virtuous, yet I am well; but till all
graces be in one woman, one woman shall not come
in my grace. Rich she shall be, that's certain; wise, or
I'll none; virtuous, or I'll never cheapen her; fair, or I'll
never look on her; mild, or come not near me; noble,
or not I for an angel; of good discourse, an excellent
musician, and her hair shall be of what colour it
please God.

*He has reached the back door -- where he sees Don Pedro, Leonato and
Claudio in the dining room.*

Ha! the prince and Monsieur Love! I will hide me in
the arbour.

He ducks around the house...

INT. DINING ROOM - DAY

All three men very clearly see Benedick avoiding them.

DON PEDRO

Come, shall we hear this music?

CLAUDIO

Yea, my good lord.

He turns on a play list, soft music underscoring their conference....

DON PEDRO

Come hither, Leonato. What was it you told me of
today, that your niece Beatrice was in love with
Signior Benedick?

*They have positioned themselves by a window -- that Benedick pops up
behind, stunned.*

CLAUDIO

I did never think that lady would have loved any man.

LEONATO

No, nor I neither; but most wonderful that she should
so dote on Signior Benedick, whom she hath in all
outward behaviors seemed ever to abhor.

CLOSE ON: BENEDICK, through the window, whispering:

BENEDICK

Is't possible? Sits the wind in that corner?

LEONATO

By my troth, my lord, I cannot tell what to think of it
but that she loves him with an enraged affection: it is
past the infinite of thought.

DON PEDRO

May be she doth but counterfeit.

CLAUDIO

Faith, like enough.

LEONATO

O God, counterfeit! There was never counterfeit
of passion came so near the life of passion as she
discovers it.

*They deliberately move to another window, which Benedick also shows
up behind, craning to hear.*

DON PEDRO

You amaze me: I would have I thought her spirit had
been invincible against all assaults of affection.

LEONATO

I would have sworn it had, my lord; especially against
Benedick.

DON PEDRO

Hath she made her affection known to Benedick?

LEONATO

No; and swears she never will: that's her torment.

CLAUDIO

'Tis true, indeed; so your daughter says: 'Shall I,' says
she, 'that have so oft encountered him with scorn,
write to him that I love him?'

LEONATO

O, she railed at herself, that she should be so
immodest to write to one that she knew would flout
her; 'I measure him,' says she, 'by my own spirit; for I
·should flout him, if he writ to me; yea, though I love
him, I should.'

CLAUDIO

Then down upon her knees she falls, weeps, sobs,
beats her heart, tears her hair, prays, curses; 'O sweet
Benedick! God give me patience!'

DON PEDRO

I would she had bestowed this dotage on me: I would
have daffed all other respects and made her half
myself. I pray you, tell Benedick of it, and hear what a'
will say.

*They start to another window -- and then double back, just to fuck with
him. He goes and returns, frustrated.*

LEONATO

Were it good, think you?

CLAUDIO

Hero thinks surely she will die; for she says she will
die, if he love her not, and she will die, ere she make
her love known, and she will die, if he woo her, rather
than she will bate one breath of her accustomed
crossness.

DON PEDRO

She doth well: if she should make tender of her love, 'tis very possible he'll scorn it; for the man, as you know all, hath a contemptible spirit.

CLAUDIO

He is a very proper man.

DON PEDRO

He hath indeed a good outward happiness.

CLAUDIO

Before God! And, in my mind, very wise.

DON PEDRO

He doth indeed show some sparks that are like wit. Well I am sorry for your niece. I love Benedick well; and I could wish he would modestly examine himself, to see how much he is unworthy so good a lady.

LEONATO

My lord, will you walk? Dinner is ready.

Exeunt DON PEDRO, CLAUDIO, and LEONATO.

EXT. BACKYARD/AMPHITHEATER - DAY

BENEDICK

[Coming forward] This can be no trick: the conference was sadly borne. They have the truth of this from Hero. Love me! Why, it must be requited. I hear how I am censured: they say I will bear myself proudly, if I perceive the love come from her; they say too that she will rather die than give any sign of affection. I did never think to marry: I must not seem proud: happy are they that hear their detractions and can put them to mending. They say the lady is fair; 'tis a truth, I can bear them witness; and virtuous; 'tis so, I cannot reprove it; and wise, but for loving me; by my troth, it is no addition to her wit, nor no great argument of her folly, for I will be horribly in love with her.

He has reached the railing, hanging on it for all the world like Leo in Titanic. He stops, turns.

BENEDICK (CONT'D)

I may chance have some odd quirks and remnants of wit broken on me, because I have railed so long against marriage: but doth not the appetite alter? A man loves the meat in his youth that he cannot endure in his age. Shall quips and sentences and these paper bullets of the brain awe a man from the career of his humour? No, the world must be peopled. When I said I would die a bachelor, I did not think I should live till I were married.

ANGLE: BEATRICE comes from the kitchen, looking a bit peeved.

BENEDICK (CONT'D)

Here comes Beatrice. By this day! she's a fair lady: I do spy some marks of love in her.

She comes to the top of the amphitheater, spying him.

BEATRICE

Against my will I am sent to bid you come in to dinner.

BENEDICK

Fair Beatrice, I thank you for your pains.

BEATRICE

I took no more pains for those thanks than you take
pains to thank me: if it had been painful, I would not
have come.

BENEDICK

You take pleasure then in the message?

BEATRICE

Yea, just so much as you may take upon a knife's point.
You have no stomach, signior: fare you well.

BEATRICE exits.

BENEDICK

Ha! 'Against my will I am sent to bid you come in to
dinner;' there's a double meaning in that 'I took no
more pains for those thanks than you took pains to
thank me.' That's as much as to say, Any pains that I
take for you is as easy as thanks. If I do not take pity of
her, I am a villain; if I do not love her, I am a fool.
(sudden excitement)
I will go get her picture.

He hurries off.

INT. KITCHEN - DAY

Beatrice re-enters. She sweeps up a basket of laundry and heads for the stairs leading below. On the other side of the kitchen, Hero and Ursula mark her and begin:

>   HERO
> No, truly, Ursula, she is too disdainful; I know her
> spirits are as coy and wild as haggerds of the rock.

>   URSULA
> But are you sure that Benedick loves Beatrice so
> entirely?

Beatrice, on the stairs, falls right out of sight. A few nasty thumps and crashes... and she reappears, peeping up just over floor level.

>   HERO
> So says the prince and my new trothed lord.

>   URSULA
> And did they bid you tell her of it, madam?

>   HERO
> They did entreat me to acquaint her of it; But I
> persuaded them, if they loved Benedick, to wish
> him wrestle with affection, And never to let Beatrice
> know of it.

URSULA

Why did you so? Doth not the gentleman deserve as
full as fortunate a bed as ever Beatrice shall couch
upon?

HERO

O god of love! I know he doth deserve As much as
may be yielded to a man: But Nature never framed
a woman's heart of prouder stuff than that of
Beatrice; Disdain and scorn ride sparkling in her eyes,
misprising what they look on, and her wit values
itself so highly that to her all matter else seems weak:
she cannot love, Nor take no shape nor project of
affection, She is so self-endeared.

URSULA

Sure, I think so; And therefore certainly it were not
good she knew his love, lest she make sport at it.

HERO

No; rather I will go to Benedick And counsel him
to fight against his passion. And, truly, I'll devise
some honest slanders To stain my cousin with: one
doth not know how much an ill word may empoison
liking.

*They move to the breakfast nook -- and here goes Beatrice, on her
knees, to get closer to hear.*

URSULA

O, do not do your cousin such a wrong. She cannot be
so much without true judgment-- Having so swift and

excellent a wit as she is prized to have--as to refuse so
rare a gentleman as Signior Benedick.

HERO

He is the only man of Italy. Always excepted my dear
Claudio. Come, go in: I'll show thee some attires,
and have thy counsel which is the best to furnish me
tomorrow.

They walk out, forcing Beatrice under the kitchen table to avoid detection. She sits up, still under there...

BEATRICE

What fire is in mine ears? Can this be true? Stand I
condemn'd for pride and scorn so much? Contempt,
farewell! And maiden pride, adieu! No glory lives
behind the back of such.

She reaches up and pulls down a bottle of wine from the table above her, swigging.

BEATRICE (CONT'D)

And, Benedick, love on; I will requite thee, taming
my wild heart to thy loving hand: If thou dost love,
my kindness shall incite thee To bind our loves up in
a holy band; For others say thou dost deserve, and I
believe it better than reportingly.

More people walk by, and she makes herself small.

EXT. LEONATO'S ESTATE - DAY

To establish.

INT. UPSTAIRS/BENEDICK'S ROOM/BATHROOM - DAY

Don Pedro and Claudio come up the stairs toward Benedick's room.

> DON PEDRO
> I do but stay till your marriage be consummate, and
> then go I toward Arragon.

> CLAUDIO
> I'll bring you thither, my lord, if you'll vouchsafe me.

> DON PEDRO
> Nay, that would be as great a soil in the new gloss of
> your marriage as to show a child his new coat and
> forbid him to wear it. I will only be bold with Benedick
> for his company; for, from the crown of his head to
> the sole of his foot, he is all mirth: he hath twice or
> thrice cut Cupid's bow-string and the little hangman
> dare not shoot at him.

*They reach Benedick's room and find him lying on his little girl bed, for
all the world like a teenage girl, legs up, newly shaven cheek on hand,
looking at Beatrice's picture.*

> BENEDICK
> Gallants, I am not as I have been.

DON PEDRO

So say I. Methinks you are sadder.

CLAUDIO

I hope he be in love.

DON PEDRO

Hang him, truant! There's no true drop of blood in him, to be truly touched with love: if he be sad, he wants money.

BENEDICK

I have the toothache.

DON PEDRO

What! Sigh for the toothache?

BENEDICK

Well, every one can master a grief but he that has it.

CLAUDIO

If he be not in love with some woman, there is no believing old signs: a' brushes his hat o'mornings; what should that bode?

Benedick rises, heading into the bathroom. They watch him at the sink, continuing:

DON PEDRO

Hath any man seen him at the barber's?

CLAUDIO

No, but the barber's man hath been seen with him,
and the old ornament of his cheek hath already
stuffed tennis-balls.

DON PEDRO

Nay, a' rubs himself with civet: can you smell him out
by that?

CLAUDIO

And when was he wont to wash his face?

DON PEDRO

Indeed, that tells a heavy tale for him: conclude,
conclude he is in love.

Leonato enters, grinning at the gaming.

CLAUDIO

Nay, but I know who loves him.

DON PEDRO

That would I know too: I warrant, one that knows him
not.

Benedick returns, glaring at his friends and ushering Leonato out into the hall.

>   BENEDICK
> Old signior, walk aside with me: I have studied eight
> or nine wise words to speak to you, which these
> hobby-horses must not hear.

INT. DON PEDRO'S ROOM - DAY

Don Pedro and Claudio enter, throwing a glance down the hall, suppressing laughter...

>   DON PEDRO
> For my life, to break with him about Beatrice.

>   CLAUDIO
> 'Tis even so. Hero and Margaret have by this played
> their parts with Beatrice; and then the two bears will
> not bite one another when they meet.

They make to look out the door again -- and Don John stands in the doorway. Everyone becomes quiet.

>   DON JOHN
> My lord and brother, God save you!

>   DON PEDRO
> Good den, brother.

DON JOHN

If your leisure served, I would speak with you.

DON PEDRO

In private?

DON JOHN

If it please you: yet Count Claudio may hear; for what I would speak of concerns him.

A beat, and Don Pedro indicates for Don John to enter.

DON PEDRO

What's the matter?

DON JOHN

[To CLAUDIO] Means your lordship to be married to-morrow?

DON PEDRO

You know he does.

DON JOHN

I know not that, when he knows what I know.

CLAUDIO

If there be any impediment, I pray you discover it.

DON JOHN

You may think I love you not: let that appear hereafter,
and aim better at me by that I now will manifest.

DON PEDRO

Why, what's the matter?

DON JOHN

The lady is disloyal.

CLAUDIO

Who, Hero?

DON PEDRO

Even she; Leonato's Hero, your Hero, every man's Hero.

Claudio slams Don John against the wall. Don John doesn't struggle, but Don Pedro peels Claudio off.

CLAUDIO

Disloyal?

DON JOHN

The word is too good to paint out her wickedness;
think you of a worse title, and I will fit her to it.
Wonder not till further warrant: go but with me to-
night, you shall see her chamber-window entered,
even the night before her wedding-day: if you love her
then, to-morrow wed her; but it would better fit your
honour to change your mind.

CLAUDIO

May this be so?

DON PEDRO

I will not think it.

DON JOHN

If you will follow me, I will show you enough; and
when you have seen more and heard more, proceed
accordingly.

The two men look at each other in disquiet.

INT. SECURITY STATION - NIGHT

*Constable DOGBERRY arrives at the station to debrief the security
team (including the two watchmen and two others). They are around
a couple of desks with blueprints and aerial photos of the estate, and
security monitors showing parts of the house. Everyone is very terse
and cop-show.*

DOGBERRY

Are you good men and true?

VERGES

Yea, or else it were pity but theyshould suffer
salvation, body andsoul.

He hands a clipboard to Dogberry.

VERGES (CONT'D)
Well, give them their charge, neighbour Dogberry.

DOGBERRY
First, who think you the most desertless man to be
constable?

FIRST WATCHMAN
Hugh Otecake, sir, or George Seacole; for they can
write and read.

DOGBERRY
Come hither, neighbour Seacole. You are thought here
to be the most senseless and fit man for the constable
of the watch; therefore bear you the lantern.

He hands the second watchman a big flashlight.

DOGBERRY (CONT'D)
This is your charge: you shall comprehend all vagrom
men; you are to bid any man stand, in the prince's
name.

SECOND WATCHMAN
How if a' will not stand?

DOGBERRY
Why, then, take no note of him, but let him go; and
presently call the rest of the watch together and thank
God you are rid of a knave.

VERGES

If he will not stand when he is bidden, he is none of
the prince's subjects.

DOGBERRY

True, and they are to meddle with none but the
prince's subjects. Well, you are to call at all the ale-
houses, and bid those that are drunk get them to bed.

SECOND WATCHMAN

How if they will not?

DOGBERRY

Why, then, let them alone till they are sober: if they
make you not then the better answer, you may say
they are not the men you took them for.

FIRST WATCHMAN

Well, sir.

DOGBERRY

If you meet a thief, you may suspect him, by virtue of
your office, to be no true man; and, for such kind of
men, the less you meddle or make with them, why the
more is for your honesty.

FIRST WATCHMAN

If we know him to be a thief, shall we not lay hands on
him?

DOGBERRY

You may; but I think they that touch pitch will be
defiled: the most peaceable way for you, if you do take
a thief, is to let him show himself what he is and steal
out of your company.

VERGES

You have been always called a merciful man, partner.

DOGBERRY

Truly, I would not hang a dog by my will, much more a
man who hath any honesty in him.

VERGES

If you hear a child cry in the night, you must call to
the nurse and bid her still it.

SECOND WATCHMAN

How if the nurse be asleep and will not hear us?

DOGBERRY

Why, then, depart in peace, and let the child wake her
with crying. This is the end of the charge: if you meet
the prince in the night, you may stay him.

VERGES

Nay, by'r our lady, that I think a' cannot.

DOGBERRY

Marry, not without the prince be willing; for, indeed,

the watch ought to offend no man; and it is an offence
to stay a man against his will.

VERGES

By'r lady, I think it be so.

DOGBERRY

Ha, ha, ha! Well, masters, good night: an there be
any matter of weight chances, call up me. Adieu: be
vigitant, I beseech you.

He and Verges exit.

FIRST WATCHMAN

Well, masters, we hear our charge: let us go sit upon
the church-bench till two, and then all to bed.

EXT. LOWER BALCONY - NIGHT

*Borachio is making his way through the dark. He's carrying a bottle
and has made his way through most of it.*

BORACHIO
(from outside)

What Conrade!

The watchmen, just stepping outside, hide behind a tool shed.

SECOND WATCHMAN
[Aside] Peace! stir not.

BORACHIO
Conrade, I say!

A match lights in the darkness -- it's Conrade, right behind him, lighting a cigarette. He starts and turns.

CONRADE
Here, man; I am at thy elbow.

BORACHIO
Mass, and my elbow itched; I thought there would a scab follow.

CONRADE
I will owe thee an answer for that: and now forward with thy tale.

BORACHIO
Stand thee close, then, and I will, like a true drunkard, utter all to thee.

FIRST WATCHMAN
(quietly)
Some treason, masters. Yet stand close.

BORACHIO

Therefore know I have earned of Don John a thousand ducats.

CONRADE

Is it possible that any villainy should be so dear?

BORACHIO

I have to-night wooed Margaret, the Lady Hero's gentlewoman, by the name of Hero:

INT. HERO'S BEDROOM - NIGHT

As tells it, we see it: Margaret and Borachio. She is putting on one Hero's dresses, laughing, nervous about being caught. He holds up another for her to try on -- one she means to be married in. Margaret looks uncertain -- do they really want to do this?

BORACHIO
(V.O.)

She leans me out at her mistress' chamber-window, bids me a thousand times good night, --

EXT. LOWER BALCONY - NIGHT

He shakes himself, continues:

BORACHIO

I tell this tale vilely: -- I should first tell thee how the prince and Claudio, planted and placed by my master

Don John, saw afar off in the orchard this
amiable encounter.

INT/EXT. HERO'S BEDROOM/BALCONY - NIGHT

*Close on Margaret, up against the doorframe in the wedding dress as
Borachio is up against her, moving rhythmically, mouthing "Hero",
Margaret looking lost and unhappy...*

CONRADE
(v.o.)
And thought they Margaret was Hero?

BORACHIO
(v.o.)
Two of them did, the prince and Claudio; but the devil
my master knew she was Margaret...

*ANGLE: THE TWO in silhouette, from far away below the balcony,
mashed together, unrecognizable...*

BORACHIO (CONT'D)
(v.o.)
... and partly by his oaths, partly by the dark night, but
chiefly by my villany, away went Claudio, enraged --

EXT. LOWER BALCONY - NIGHT

BORACHIO
-- swore he would meet her next morning at the
temple, and there, before the whole congregation,

shame her with what he saw o'er night and send her
home again without a husband.

The watchmen rush out, guns drawn. Nervous but firm.

FIRST WATCHMAN
We charge you, in the prince's name, stand!

SECOND WATCHMAN
(into a walkie talkie)
Call up the right master constable. We have here
recovered the most dangerous piece of lechery that
ever was known in the commonwealth.

CONRADE
(sweetly)
Masters, masters...

FIRST WATCHMAN
(pulls back the hammer)
Never speak: we charge you let us obey you to go with
us.

Conrade and Borachio look at each other -- busted. By morons.

EXT. BACKYARD/ATRIUM - DAY

*We see the photographer setting up and Leonato's Aide overseeing the
household staff decorate for the wedding..*

INT. DINING ROOM - DAY

As the table is laid out by Ursula amd the house staff.

INT. HERO'S BEDROOM CLOSET – DAY

Hero has pulled out the dress that Margaret wore last night. Margaret looks nervous as Hero examines it.

                    MARGARET
        Troth, I think your other gown were better.

                    HERO
        No, pray thee, good Meg, I'll wear this.

                    MARGARET
        By my troth, 's not so good; and I warrant your cousin
        will say so.

                    HERO
        My cousin's a fool, and thou art another: I'll wear
        none but this.

Enter BEATRICE, distracted. Hero hands the dress to Margaret, who lays it aside, pulling out a veil, gloves, various distractions...

                    HERO (CONT'D)
        Good morrow, coz.

BEATRICE
(sinks into a chair)
Good morrow, sweet Hero.

HERO
Why how now? Do you speak in the sick tune?

She throws a knowing grin at Margaret.

BEATRICE
I am out of all other tune, methinks. 'Tis almost five
o'clock, cousin; tis time you were ready. By my troth, I
am exceeding ill: heighho!

MARGARET
(hands gloves to Hero)
For a hawk, a horse, or a husband?

HERO
These gloves the count sent me; they are an excellent
perfume.

BEATRICE
I am stuffed, cousin; I cannot smell.

MARGARET
A maid, and stuffed! There's goodly catching of cold.

BEATRICE

By my troth, I am sick.

MARGARET

Get you some of this distilled Carduus Benedictus, and
lay it to your heart: it is the only thing for a qualm.

BEATRICE

Benedictus! Why Benedictus? You have some moral in
this Benedictus.

MARGARET

Moral! No, by my troth, I have no moral meaning; I
meant, plain holy-thistle.

HERO
(aside, to Margaret)
There thou prickest her with a thistle.

Ursula enters.

URSULA

Madam, withdraw: the prince, the count,
(pointedly, for Beatrice)
Signior Benedick, Don John, and all the gallants of the
town, are come to fetch you to church.

*Hero and the two others give an excited squeal, start dressing her
quickly. Beatrice rises, checking her hair and outfit nervously.*

EXT. SIDE ALLEY BY LEONATO'S ESTATE - DAY

Dogberry and Verges face Leonato and His Aide.

LEONATO

What would you with me, honest neighbour?

DOGBERRY

Marry, sir, I would have some confidence with you that decerns you nearly.

LEONATO

Brief, I pray you; for you see it is a busy time with me.

DOGBERRY

Marry, this it is, sir.

VERGES

Yes, in truth it is, sir.

LEONATO

What is it, my good friends?

DOGBERRY

Goodman Verges, sir, speaks alittle off the matter: his wits are not so blunt as, God help, I woulddesire they were; but, in faith, honest as the skin between his brows.

VERGES

Yes, I thank God I am as honest as any man living.

DOGBERRY

Comparisons are odorous.

LEONATO

Neighbours, you are tedious.

DOGBERRY

It pleases your worship to say so, but we are the poor duke's officers.

LEONATO

I would fain know what you have to say.

VERGES

Marry, sir, our watch to-night, excepting your worship's presence, ha' ta'en a couple of as arrant knaves as any in Messina.

DOGBERRY

A good old man, sir; he will be talking: God help us! Well said, neighbour Verges; an two men ride of a horse, one must ride behind.

LEONATO

I must leave you.

DOGBERRY

One word, sir: our watch, sir, have indeed
comprehended two aspicious persons, and we would
have them this morning examined before your
worship.

LEONATO

Take their examination yourself and bring it me: I am
now in great haste, as it may appear unto you.

DOGBERRY

It shall be suffigance.

AIDE

Drink some wine ere you go.

*They move off toward the backyard. Dogberry and Verges watch
them.*

DOGBERRY

Go, good partner, go: we are now to examination
these men.

They head towards the front.

EXT. BACKYARD/ATRIUM - DAY

*Leonato leads Hero down the stone steps to the atrium, where FRIAR
FRANCIS waits with a stone-faced Claudio, Don Pedro equally grave by
his side.*

The other guests stand on the various steps, watching. Benedick is near the back, eyes on:

BEATRICE, in the atrium, who looks around just as he ducks back.

FRIAR FRANCIS
You come hither, my lord, to marry this lady.

CLAUDIO
No.

LEONATO
To be married to her: friar, you come to marry her.

FRIAR FRANCIS
Lady, you come hither to be married to this count.

HERO
I do.

FRIAR FRANCIS
If either of you know any inward impediment why you should not be conjoined, charge you, on your souls, to utter it.

CLAUDIO
Know you any, Hero?

HERO

None, my lord.

FRIAR FRANCIS

Know you any, count?

LEONATO

I dare make his answer, none.

CLAUDIO

O, what men dare do! What men may do! What men daily do, not knowing what they do!

There is awkward silence. Benedick tries to be useful:

BENEDICK

How now! Interjections? Why, then, some be of laughing, as, ah, ha, he!

Yeah, crickets. He slinks off to the open bar behind him.

CLAUDIO

Stand thee by, friar. Father, by your leave: Will you with free and unconstrained soul Give me this maid, your daughter?

LEONATO

As freely, son, as God did give her me.

CLAUDIO

And what have I to give you back, whose worth may counterpoise this rich and precious gift?

DON PEDRO

Nothing, unless you render her again.

CLAUDIO

Sweet prince, you learn me noble thankfulness.

He roughly pushes Hero toward Leonato.

CLAUDIO (CONT'D)

There, Leonato, take her back again: Give not this rotten orange to your friend; She's but the sign and
. semblance of her honour.
(to the crowd)
Behold how like a maid she blushes here! Would you not swear, All you that see her, that she were a maid, By these exterior shows? But she is none: She knows the heat of a luxurious bed; Her blush is guiltiness, not modesty.

*Beatrice starts forward, but a hard gesture from Leonato stops her --
he'll handle this.*

LEONATO

What do you mean, my lord?

139

CLAUDIO

Not to be married, Not to knit my soul to an approved wanton.

LEONATO

(taking Claudio aside)

Dear my lord, if you, in your own proof, Have vanquish'd the resistance of her youth, And made defeat of her virginity,-

CLAUDIO

(loudly)

I know what you would say: if I have known her, You will say she did embrace me as a husband, And so extenuate the 'forehand sin: No, Leonato, I never tempted her with word too large; But, as a brother to his sister, show'd Bashful sincerity and comely love.

HERO

And seem'd I ever otherwise to you?

CLAUDIO

Out on thee! Seeming! I will write against it: You seem to me as Dian in her orb, As chaste as is the bud ere it be blown; But you are more intemperate in your blood than Venus, or those pamper'd animals that rage in savage sensuality.

HERO

Is my lord well, that he doth speak so wide?

LEONATO

Sweet prince, why speak not you?

DON PEDRO

What should I speak? I stand dishonour'd, that have gone about To link my dear friend to a common stale.

A gasp from the crowd. Benedick has returned with a drink, is taking in the scene:

BENEDICK

This looks not like a nuptial.

CLAUDIO

What man was he talk'd with you yesternight out at your window betwixt twelve and one? Now, if you are a maid, answer to this.

HERO

I talk'd with no man at that hour, my lord.

DON PEDRO

Why, then are you no maiden. Leonato, I am sorry you must hear: upon mine honour, myself, my brother and this grieved count did see her, hear her, at that hour last night talk with a ruffian at her chamber-window who hath indeed, most like a liberal villain, Confess'd the vile encounters they have had a thousand times in secret.

DON JOHN
(from the steps)
Fie, fie! They are not to be named, my lord, not to be
spoke of; there is not chastity enough in language
Without offence to utter them. Thus, pretty lady, I am
sorry for thy much misgovernment.

CLAUDIO
O Hero, what a Hero hadst thou been, If half thy
outward graces had been placed About thy thoughts
and counsels of thy heart! But fare thee well, most
foul, most fair!

*He starts up the steps, Don Pedro beside him. They fall in with Don
John.*

LEONATO
Hath no man's dagger here a point for me?

HERO swoons.

BEATRICE
Why, how now, cousin! Wherefore sink you down?

DON JOHN
Come, let us go. These things, come thus to light,
Smother her spirits up.

*Exeunt DON PEDRO, DON JOHN, and CLAUDIO. Benedick moves
toward the atrium.*

BENEDICK

How doth the lady?

BEATRICE

Dead, I think. Help, uncle! Hero! why, Hero! Signior
Benedick!

*Benedick approaches, but Leonato roughly pushes him back. The other
guests are fading back, awkward or appalled. The Aide is ushering
them away, also pulling the photographer from the scene.*

LEONATO

O Fate! Take not away thy heavy hand. Death is the
fairest cover for her shame That may be wish'd for.

BEATRICE

How now, cousin Hero!

FRIAR FRANCIS

Have comfort, lady.

Hero comes to, looks about wildly.

LEONATO

Dost thou look up?

FRIAR FRANCIS

Yea, wherefore should she not?

LEONATO

Wherefore! Why, doth not every earthly thing cry
shame upon her? Could she here deny the story that
is printed in her blood? Do not live, Hero; do not ope
thine eyes. Grieved I, I had but one? Chid I for that at
frugal nature's frame? O, one too much by thee! Why
had I one? Why ever wast thou lovely in my eyes?

BENEDICK

Sir, sir, be patient. For my part, I am so attired in
wonder, I know not what to say.

BEATRICE

O, on my soul, my cousin is belied!

BENEDICK

Lady, were you her bedfellow last night?

BEATRICE

No, truly not; although, until last night, I have this
twelvemonth been her bedfellow.

LEONATO

Confirm'd, confirm'd! Would the two princes lie, and
Claudio lie, who loved her so, that, speaking of her
foulness, wash'd it with tears? Hence from her! Let her
die.

FRIAR FRANCIS

Lady, what man is he you are accused of?

HERO

They know that do accuse me; I know none: If I know
more of any man alive than that which maiden
modesty doth warrant, Let all my sins lack mercy! O
my father, Prove you that any man with me conversed
at hours unmeet, or that I yesternight maintain'd the
change of words with any creature, refuse me, hate
me, torture me to death!

*Leonato embraces his daughter almost as roughly as he rejected her,
still looking about, eyes wet.*

FRIAR FRANCIS

There is some strange misprision in the princes.

BENEDICK

Two of them have the very bent of honour; And if
their wisdoms be misled in this, the practise of it
lives in John the bastard, whose spirits toil in frame of
villanies.

Leonato clutches his daughter, half in love, half in wrath.

LEONATO

I know not. If they speak but truth of her, These hands
shall tear her; if they wrong her honour, The proudest
of them shall well hear of it.

FRIAR FRANCIS

Pause awhile, And let my counsel sway you in this
case. Your daughter here the princes left for dead: Let

her awhile be secretly kept in, And publish it that she
is dead indeed.

LEONATO

What shall become of this? What will this do?

FRIAR FRANCIS

When Claudio shall hear she died upon his words,
The idea of her life shall sweetly creep into his study
of imagination, and every lovely organ of her life
shall come apparell'd in more precious habit, more
moving-delicate and full of life, into the eye and
prospect of his soul, than when she lived indeed; then
shall he mourn, if ever love had interest in his liver,
and wish he had not so accused her, No, though he
thought his accusation true.

BENEDICK

Signior Leonato, let the friar advise you.

LEONATO

Being that I flow in grief, The smallest twine may lead
me.

*Benedick leads Leonato off, as Beatrice tends to Hero. He looks at her,
but she doesn't see.*

FRIAR FRANCIS

Come, lady, die to live: this wedding-day Perhaps is
but prolong'd.

INT. DINING ROOM - DAY

Beatrice sits at the lavishly set table, weeping quietly, as Benedick enters.

BENEDICK
Lady Beatrice, have you wept all this while?

BEATRICE
(turning away)
Yea, and I will weep a while longer.

BENEDICK
I will not desire that.

BEATRICE
You have no reason; I do it freely.

BENEDICK
Surely I do believe your fair cousin is wronged.

BEATRICE
Ah, how much might the man deserve of me that would right her!

BENEDICK
Is there any way to show such friendship?

BEATRICE

A very even way, but no such friend.

She stands, moving away toward the French doors. He follows.

BENEDICK

May a man do it?

BEATRICE

It is a man's office, but not yours.

BENEDICK

I do love nothing in the world so well as you: is not
that strange?

BEATRICE
(turns almost to face him)
As strange as the thing I know not. It were as possible
for me to say I loved nothing so well as you: but
believe me not; and yet I lie not; I confess nothing, nor
I deny nothing. I am sorry for my cousin.

BENEDICK

By my sword, Beatrice, thou lovest me.

BEATRICE

Do not swear, and eat it.

BENEDICK

I will swear by it that you love me; and I will make him
eat it that says I love not you.

BEATRICE

Will you not eat your word?

BENEDICK

With no sauce that can be devised to it. I protest I love
thee.

BEATRICE

Why, then, God forgive me!

BENEDICK

What offence, sweet Beatrice?

BEATRICE

You have stayed me in a happy hour: I was about to
protest I loved you.

BENEDICK

And do it with all thy heart.

BEATRICE

I love you with so much of my heart that none is left
to protest.

They kiss, fiercely. Hold each other close, his face buried in her neck...

BENEDICK
Come, bid me do any thing for thee.

BEATRICE
Kill Claudio.

He moves back, looking at her with suspicious disbelief.

BENEDICK
Ha! Not for the wide world.

BEATRICE
(pushing past him)
You kill me to deny it. Farewell.

BENEDICK
Tarry, sweet Beatrice.

BEATRICE
I am gone, though I am here: there is no love in you:
nay, I pray you, let me go.

BENEDICK
Beatrice,-

BEATRICE

In faith, I will go.

BENEDICK

We'll be friends first.

She wrests free of his grasp and turns on him.

BEATRICE

You dare easier be friends with me than fight with
mine enemy.

BENEDICK

Is Claudio thine enemy?

BEATRICE

Is he not approved in the height a villain, that hath
slandered, scorned, dishonoured my kinswoman? O
that I were a man! What, bear her in hand until they
come to take hands; and then, with public accusation,
uncovered slander, unmitigated rancour, -- O God,
that I were a man! I would eat his heart in the market-
place.

BENEDICK

Hear me, Beatrice,-

BEATRICE

Talk with a man out at a window! A proper saying!

BENEDICK

Nay, but, Beatrice,-

BEATRICE

Sweet Hero! She is wronged, she is slandered, she is undone.

BENEDICK

Beat-

BEATRICE

Princes and counties! O that I were a man for his sake! Or that I had any friend would be a man for my sake!

She moves to the bar, shakily trying to pour a whiskey, which she does not drink.

BEATRICE (CONT'D)

But manhood is melted into courtesies, valour into compliment, and men are only turned into tongue: he is now as valiant as Hercules that only tells a lie and swears it. I cannot be a man with wishing, therefore I will die a woman with grieving.

BENEDICK

Tarry, good Beatrice. By this hand, I love thee.

BEATRICE

Use it for my love some other way than swearing by it.

BENEDICK

Think you in your soul the Count Claudio hath
wronged Hero?

BEATRICE

Yea, as sure as I have a thought or a soul.

BENEDICK

Enough, I am engaged; I will challenge him. I will kiss
your hand, and so I leave you. By this hand, Claudio
shall render me a dear account. As you hear of me, so
think of me. Go, comfort your cousin: I must say she is
dead: and so, farewell.

He leaves.

INT. INTERROGATION ROOM - DAY

*Conrade and Borachio sit at a table to one side of the room. At the
other, Verges watches with the SEXTON -- in essence, the D.A. -- a
businesslike woman with a pad and a thick case-file. Dogberry has his
jacket off, rolled up sleeves -- paces by the table. Tension is high.*

DOGBERRY

What is your name, friend?

BORACHIO

Borachio.

DOGBERRY

Pray, write down, Borachio. Yours, sirrah?

CONRADE

My name is Conrade.

DOGBERRY

Masters, do you serve God?

CONRADE

Yea, sir, we hope.

DOGBERRY

Write down, that they hope they serve God: and write
God first; for God defend but God should go before
such villains! Masters, it is proved already that you are
little better than false knaves; and it will go near to be
thought so shortly. How answer you for yourselves?

CONRADE

Marry, sir, we say we are none.

Dogberry crosses to Verges, confides:

DOGBERRY

A marvellous witty fellow, I assure you: but I will go
about with him.

He crosses back to the table, leans in toward Borachio.

DOGBERRY (CONT'D)

A word in your ear: sir, I say to you, it is thought you
are false knaves.

BORACHIO

Sir, I say to you we are none.

DOGBERRY

Well, stand aside.
                    (to Verges, frustrated)
'Fore God, they are both in a tale.
                    (to the Sexton)
Have you writ down, that they are none?

SEXTON

Master constable, you go not the way to examine: you
must call forth the watch that are their accusers.

*Verges opens a door and the two watchmen enter. He circles toward the
table as they come near the Sexton.*

VERGES

Masters, I charge you, in the prince's name, accuse
these men.

FIRST WATCHMAN

This man said, sir, that Don John, the prince's
brother, was a villain.

DOGBERRY

Write down Prince John a villain. Why, this is flat
perjury, to call a prince's brother villain.

BORACHIO

Master constable,-

DOGBERRY

Pray thee, fellow, peace: I do not like thy look, I
promise thee.

SEXTON

What heard you him say else?

SECOND WATCHMAN

Marry, that he had received a thousand ducats of Don
John for accusing the Lady Hero wrongfully.

DOGBERRY

Flat burglary as ever was committed.

*Verges slams a hand on the table, suddenly playing the wild card, right
in their faces:*

VERGES

Yea, by mass, that it is.

*Dogberry throws him a look, and he backs off -- but he's a loose
cannon, that Verges...*

SEXTON

What else, fellow?

FIRST WATCHMAN

And that Count Claudio did mean, upon his words, to disgrace Hero before the whole assembly, and not marry her.

DOGBERRY

O villain! Thou wilt be condemned into everlasting redemption for this.

SEXTON

What else?

FIRST WATCHMAN

This is all.

The Sexton starts putting away her things, preparing to go.

SEXTON

And this is more, masters, than you can deny. Prince John is this morning secretly stolen away; Hero was in this manner accused, in this very manner refused, and upon the grief of this suddenly died.

ANGLE: BORACHIO is stunned by this news.

SEXTON (CONT'D)
Master constable, let these men be bound, and
brought to Leonato's: I will go before and show him
their examination.

SEXTON exits.

DOGBERRY
Come, let them be opinioned.

*Verges and the others move to cuff them. Borachio does not struggle,
but Conrade -*

VERGES
Let them be in the hands-

*-- slams Verges' head into the table, as the other two grab
her.*

CONRADE
Off, coxcomb!

DOGBERRY
God's my life, where's the sexton? Let him write down
the prince's officer coxcomb. Come, bind them. Thou
naughty varlet!

CONRADE
Away! You are an ass, you are an ass.

Everyone is silent, as Dogberry gets in Conrade's face.

DOGBERRY

Dost thou not suspect my place? Dost thou not suspect
my years? O that she were here to write me down an
ass! But, masters, remember that I am an ass; though
it be not written down, yet forget not that I am an ass.
Thou villain!

*They start taking them out, Dogberry continuing, increasingly loud, as
he rolls down his sleeves:*

DOGBERRY (CONT'D)

I am a wise fellow, and, which is more, an officer, and,
which is more, a householder, and, which is more, as
pretty a piece of flesh as any is in Messina, and one
that knows the law, go to; and a rich fellow enough,
go to; and a fellow that hath had losses, and one that
hath two gowns and every thing handsome about him.
(grabbing his jacket)
O that I had been writ down an ass!

INT. LIBRARY - DAY

*Claudio and Don Pedro enter to find Benedick looking out the front
window.*

CLAUDIO

Now, signior, what news?

BENEDICK
Good day, my lord.

CLAUDIO
We have been up and down to seek thee; for we are
high-proof melancholy and would fain have it beaten
away. Wilt thou use thy wit?

He turns, his eyes cold.

BENEDICK
(showing his gun)
It is in my scabbard: shall I drawit?

DON PEDRO
(uncertain)
Dost thou wear thy wit by thy side?

CLAUDIO
Never any did so, though very many have been beside
their wit. I will bid thee draw, as we do the minstrels;
draw, to pleasure us.

DON PEDRO
As I am an honest man, he looks pale. Art thou sick,
or angry?

CLAUDIO
What, courage, man! What though care killed a cat,
thou hast mettle enough in thee to kill care.

DON PEDRO

But when shall we set the savage bull's horns on the sensible Benedick's head?

CLAUDIO

Yea, and text underneath, 'Here dwells Benedick the married man'?

BENEDICK

Shall I speak a word in your ear?

CLAUDIO

God bless me from a challenge!

Benedick SLAPS Claudio hard.

BENEDICK

You are a villain; I jest not: I will make it good how you dare, with what you dare, and when you dare. Do me right, or I will protest your cowardice.

CLAUDIO

Well, I will meet you, so I may have good cheer.

BENEDICK

My lord, for your many courtesies I thank you: I must discontinue your company: your brother the bastard is fled from Messina: you have among you killed a sweet and innocent lady. For my Lord Lackbeard there, he and I shall meet: and, till then, peace be with him.

He leaves, Don Pedro watching him...

DON PEDRO
Did he not say, my brother was fled?

A noise makes them look out the front window:

EXT. FRONT YARD - DAY

Dogberry and Verges pull Borachio and Conrade up the walk as Don Pedro and Claudio step out from the courtyard.

DON PEDRO
Officers, what offence have these men done?

DOGBERRY
Marry, sir, they have committed false report;
moreover, they have spoken untruths; secondarily,
they are slanders; sixth and lastly, they have belied a
lady; thirdly, they have verified unjust things; and, to
conclude, they are lying knaves.

DON PEDRO
(To Conrade)
This learned constable is too cunning to be
understood: what's your offence?

BORACHIO
Sweet prince, let me go no farther to mine answer:
do you hear me, and let this count kill me. I have

deceived even your very eyes: what your wisdoms
could not discover, these shallow fools have brought
to light: who overheard me confessing how your
brother incensed me to slander the Lady Hero, how
you saw me court Margaret in Hero's garments, how
you disgraced her: my villany they have upon record;
which I had rather seal with my death than repeat
over to my shame.

DON PEDRO
Runs not this speech like iron through your blood?

CLAUDIO
I have drunk poison whiles he utter'd it.

DOGBERRY
Come, bring away the plaintiffs: by this time our
sexton hath reformed Signior Leonato of the matter:
and, masters, do not forget to specify, when time and
place shall serve, that I am an ass.

Leonato comes out the front gate with the Sexton.

LEONATO
Which is the villain? Let me see his eyes, that, when I
note another man like him, I may avoid him: which of
these is he?

BORACHIO
If you would know your wronger, look on me.

LEONATO

Art thou the slave that with thy breath hast kill'd
mine innocent child?

BORACHIO

Yea, even I alone.

LEONATO

No, not so, villain: Here stand a pair of honourable
men; A third is fled, that had a hand in it. I thank you,
princes, for my daughter's death: Record it with your
high and worthy deeds: 'Twas bravely done, if you
bethink you of it.

CLAUDIO

I know not how to pray your patience; Yet I must
speak. Choose your revenge yourself; impose me to
what penance your invention Can lay upon my sin: yet
sinn'd I not but in mistaking.

DON PEDRO

By my soul, nor I: And yet, to satisfy this good old man,
I would bend under any heavy weight That he'll enjoin
me to.

LEONATO

I cannot bid you bid my daughter live; That were
impossible: but, I pray you both, possess the people
in Messina here how innocent she died; and if your
love can labour ought in sad invention, hang her
an epitaph upon her tomb and sing it to her bones,
sing it to-night: To-morrow morning come you to my

house, and since you could not be my son-in-law, be yet my nephew: my brother hath a daughter, almost the copy of my child that's dead, And she alone is heir to both of us: Give her the right you should have given her cousin, and so dies my revenge.

CLAUDIO

I do embrace your offer; and dispose for henceforth of poor Claudio.

LEONATO

(looks at Borachio)

This naughty man shall face to face be brought to Margaret, who I believe was pack'd in all this wrong, hired to it by your brother.

BORACHIO

No, by my soul, she was not, Nor knew not what she did when she spoke to me, but always hath been just and virtuous In any thing that I do know by her.

DOGBERRY

Moreover, sir, which indeed is not under white and black, this plaintiff here, the offender, did call me ass: I beseech you, let it be remembered in his punishment.

LEONATO

I thank thee for thy care and honest pains.

DOGBERRY

God keep your worship! I humbly give you leave to depart; and if a merry meeting may bewished, God prohibit it! Come, neighbor.

Exeunt DOGBERRY and VERGES.

LEONATO

Until to-morrow morning, lords, farewell.

DON PEDRO

We will not fail.

LEONATO

[To the Watch] Bring you these fellows on. We'll talk with Margaret, how her acquaintance grew with this lewd fellow.

INT. UPSTAIRS/BENEDICK'S ROOM - DAY

Margaret is pulling dead flowers from a vase by Hero's room, looking nervous and unhappy. She puts them in a basket with others, moving past Benedick's room, where he, looking nervous as well and holding a piece of paper, accosts her:

BENEDICK

Pray thee, sweet Mistress Margaret, deserve well at my hands by helping me to the speech of Beatrice.

MARGARET
(sad smile)
Will you then write me a sonnet in praise of my
beauty?

Seeing her upset, he moves to her, kindly:

BENEDICK
In so high a style, Margaret, that no man living shall
come over it; for, in most comely truth, thou deservest
it.

MARGARET
(trying to be game)
To have no man come over me! Why, shall I always
keep below stairs?

BENEDICK
Thy wit is as quick as the greyhound's mouth; it
catches.

MARGARET
And yours as blunt as the fencer's foils, which hit, but
hurt not.

BENEDICK
A most manly wit, Margaret; it will not hurt a woman:
and so, I pray thee, call Beatrice: I give thee the
bucklers.

MARGARET
Give us the swords; we have bucklers of our own.

She exits, and he moves out to:

EXT. BALCONY/FRONT COUTYARD - DAY

He hums a bit, looking at his paper, then sings:

BENEDICK (CONT.)
The god of love,
That sits above,
And knows me,
and knows me,
How pitiful I deserve,-
(giving up)
I mean in singing; but in loving, Leander the good
swimmer, Troilus the first employer of panders, why,
they were never so truly turned over and over as my
poor self in love. Marry, I cannot show it in rhyme; I
have tried: I can find out no rhyme to 'lady' but 'baby,'
an innocent rhyme; for 'scorn,' 'horn,' a hard rhyme;
for 'school,' 'fool,' a babbling rhyme; very ominous
endings: no, I was not born under a rhyming planet,
nor I cannot woo in festival terms.

*He hears Beatrice approaching and scurries down to the bottom of the
stair-case, the better to play a true balcony scene with her.*

BENEDICK (CONT.) (CONT'D)
Sweet Beatrice, wouldst thou come when I called thee?

BEATRICE

Yea, signior, and depart when you bid me.

BENEDICK

O, stay but till then!

BEATRICE

'Then' is spoken; fare you well now: and yet, ere I go,
let me go with that I came; which is, with knowing
what hath passed between you and Claudio.

BENEDICK
(running back up)
Only foul words; and thereupon I will kiss thee.

BEATRICE

Foul words is but foul wind, and foul wind is but foul
breath, and foul breath is noisome; therefore I will
depart unkissed.

BENEDICK

Thou hast frighted the word out of his right sense, so
forcible is thy wit. But I must tell thee plainly, Claudio
undergoes my challenge; and either I must shortly
hear from him, or I will subscribe him a coward.

She brings him in for a true kiss. He settles back on the balcony...

BENEDICK (CONT'D)

And, I pray thee now, tell me for which of my bad
parts didst thou first fall in love with me?

BEATRICE

For them all together; which maintained so politic a
state of evil that they will not admit any good part to
intermingle with them. But for which of my good parts
did you first suffer love for me?

BENEDICK

Suffer love! a good epithet! I do suffer love indeed, for
I love thee against my will.

BEATRICE

In spite of your heart, I think; alas, poor heart! If you
spite it for my sake, I will spite it for yours; for I will
never love that which my friend hates.

BENEDICK

Thou and I are too wise to woo peaceably. And now
tell me, how doth your cousin?

BEATRICE

Very ill.

BENEDICK

And how do you?

BEATRICE

Very ill too.

BENEDICK

Serve God, love me and mend.

Ursula runs into the courtyard, calls up to them:

URSULA

Madam, you must come to your uncle. It is proved my
Lady Hero hath been falsely accused, the prince and
Claudio mightily abused; and Don John is the author
of all, who is fled and gone. Will you come presently?

BEATRICE

Will you go hear this news, signior?

BENEDICK

I will live in thy heart, die in thy lap, and be buried
in thy eyes; and moreover I will go with thee to thy
uncle's.

EXT. LOWER WOODS - NIGHT

*We see a procession by candle-light, led by Claudio and Don Pedro,
down towards the family crypt. Over, a haunting song of regret.*

*ANGLE: HERO, out of sight, looks down from the balcony, watching
Claudio, some steel in her eyes, but some sympathy too. She turns to
Beatrice, who puts her arm around her.*

ANGLE: CLAUDIO, genuinely mournful.

FRIAR FRANCIS
(V.O.)
Did I not tell you she was innocent?

INT. LIVING ROOM - DAY

As the Friar, Leonato, and Benedick prepare for the ceremony.

ANGLE: UPSTAIRS, we see the women donning veils, including Margaret and Ursula. Hero is gently adjusting Margaret's.

LEONATO
So are the prince and Claudio, who accused her upon the error that you heard debated:
(calling up)
But Margaret was in some fault for this -
(Hero glares at him)
-- although against her will, as it appears in the true course of all the question.

FRIAR FRANCIS
Well, I am glad that all things sort so well.

The women retreat. Benedick takes the Friar aside.

BENEDICK
Friar, I must entreat your pains, I think.

FRIAR FRANCIS

To do what, signior?

BENEDICK

To bind me, or undo me; one of them. Signior
Leonato, truth it is, good signior, your niece regards
me with an eye of favour.

LEONATO

That eye my daughter lent her: 'tis most true.

BENEDICK

And I do with an eye of love requite her.

LEONATO

The sight whereof I think you had from me, From
Claudio and the prince: but what's your will?

BENEDICK

Your answer, sir, is enigmatical: But, for my will, my
will is your good will may stand with ours, this day to
be conjoin'd In the state of honourable marriage: In
which, good friar, I shall desire your help.

EXT. BACKYARD - DAY

*All are assembled near the archway where the Friar and Leonato
stand, the women behind them -- a much sparser, and sparsely
attended, gathering. Don Pedro and Claudio make their way through
the guests.*

DON PEDRO

Good morrow to this fair assembly.

LEONATO

Good morrow, prince; good morrow, Claudio: We here attend you. Are you yet determined To-day to marry with my brother's daughter?

CLAUDIO

I'll hold my mind, were she an Ethiope.

Benedick looks at him, slightly stupified.

LEONATO

Call her forth; here's the friar ready.

The veiled women step forward.

CLAUDIO

Which is the lady I must seize upon?

LEONATO

This same is she, and I do give you her.

CLAUDIO

Why, then she's mine. Sweet, let me see your face.

LEONATO

No, that you shall not, till you take her hand Before
this friar and swear to marry her.

CLAUDIO

Give me your hand: before this holy friar, I am your
husband, if you like of me.

HERO

And when I lived, I was your other wife:

Unmasking...

HERO (CONT'D)

And when you loved, you were my other husband.

CLAUDIO

Another Hero!

HERO

Nothing certainer: One Hero died defiled, but I do
live, and surely as I live -
(steely)
-- I am a maid.

*Hand in hers, her goes down on his knees, head down. She touches his
hair with rueful affection.*

DON PEDRO

The former Hero! Hero that is –
                    (shooting Leonato a look)
-- dead!

LEONATO

She died, my lord, but whiles her slander lived.

FRIAR FRANCIS

All this amazement can I qualify: When after that the
holy rites are ended, I'll tell you largely of fair Hero's
death: Meantime let wonder seem familiar, And to the
chapel let us presently.

BENEDICK

Soft and fair, friar. Which is Beatrice?

BEATRICE

[Unmasking] I answer to that name. What is your will?

BENEDICK

Do not you love me?

BEATRICE

Why, no; no more than reason.

BENEDICK

Why, then your uncle and the prince and Claudio have
been deceived; they swore you did.

Hero whispers in Claudio's ear. He grins, and they slip away into the house.

BEATRICE

Do not you love me?

BENEDICK

Troth, no; no more than reason.

BEATRICE

Why, then my cousin Margaret and Ursula are much deceived; for they did swear you did.

BENEDICK

They swore that you were almost sick for me.

BEATRICE

They swore that you were well-nigh dead for me.

BENEDICK

'Tis no such matter. Then you do not love me?

BEATRICE

No, truly, but in friendly recompense.

LEONATO

Come, cousin, I am sure you love the gentleman.

Claudio appears on the balcony from Hero's room, tossing a piece of paper down at them, which Benedick tries – but fails -- to snatch before Beatrice does.

CLAUDIO
And I'll be sworn upon't that he loves her; for here's a paper written in his hand, a halting sonnet of his own pure brain, Fashion'd to Beatrice.

Hero joins him, tossing out another -- Beatrice is too busy reading to see it in time, and only manages to kick Benedick in the shins because he got it first.

HERO
And here's another writ in my cousin's hand, stolen from her pocket, containing her affection unto Benedick.

They both read.

BENEDICK
A miracle! Here's our own hands against our hearts. Come, I will have thee; but, by this light, I take thee for pity.

BEATRICE
I would not deny you; but, by this good day, I yield upon great persuasion; and partly to save your life, for I was told you were in a consumption.

BENEDICK
Peace! I will stop your mouth.

Benedick kisses Beatrice. Claudio and Hero watch from above, as he folds her into his arms. Don Pedro cannot resist:

DON PEDRO
How dost thou, Benedick, the married man?

BENEDICK
I'll tell thee what, prince; a college of wit-crackers cannot flout me out of my humour. Dost thou think I care for a satire or an epigram? No: since I do purpose to marry, I will think nothing to any purpose that the world can say against it; and therefore never flout at me for what I have said against it; for man is a giddy thing, and this is my conclusion.

Leonato's Aide steps forward, reading from his phone:

AIDE
(to Do Pedro)
My lord, your brother John is ta'en in flight, And brought with armed men back to Messina.

He shows Don Pedro and the others:

ANGLE: ON THE PHONE is a TMZ-style, long lens photo of Don John being shackled by none other than Dogberry and Verges.

BENEDICK
Think not on him till to-morrow: I'll devise thee brave
punishments for him.

As they move toward the house -

BENEDICK (CONT'D)
Let's have a dance ere we are married, that we may
lighten our own hearts and our wives' heels.

LEONATO
We'll have dancing afterward.

BENEDICK
First, of my word; therefore play, music.
(to Don Pedro)
Prince, thou art sad; get thee a wife...
(to Beatrice, enraptured)
...get thee a wife.

MUSIC OVER:

INT. DINING ROOM - NIGHT

*The room has been cleared and is filled with dancers, the party once
again going long into the night.*

*ANGLE: BEATRICE AND BENEDICK stand together in the archway,
close, not dancing with those in the background, just looking, a hand in
the hair, on the shoulder, foreheads touching, lost in wonder and sweet
relief.*

THE
END

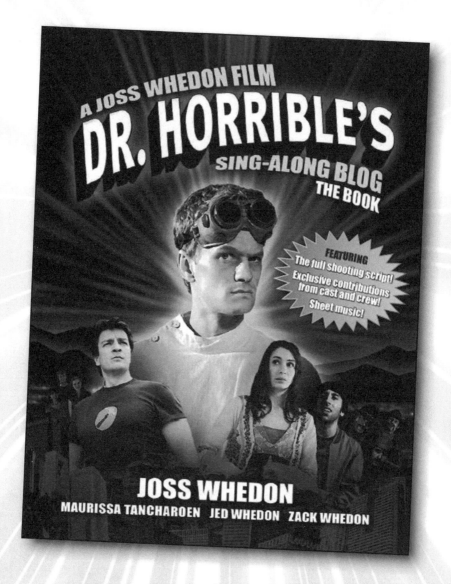